Enigma Thrillers

Also published by Enigma Books

Benoît Séverac

Pax Romana

Murder in Aquitania

Translated by Catherine E. Dop-Miller

Enigma Books

Originally published by éditions TME - Toulouse, France
in the series *noire d'Histoire* under the title:
Les Chevelues

Translated by Catherine E. Dop-Miller

First English Edition

ISBN 978-1-929631-97-1
e-ISBN 978-1-936274-17-8

Pax Romana

Murder in Aquitania

I

The cool, almost cold air hit him in the chest. A little steam rose off his white tunic, and lifted from his horse. His tunic was white, just like his horse. He breathed deeply, taking in the voluptuous shape of the Pyrenees stretching before him. Cracius sat up in his saddle, his thighs still sore from the night's exertions, completely spent but intoxicated by victory. He felt supreme: he felt taller than the oak at the top of the hill where he stopped every time he returned from a night of love making. The hill was his domain; it overlooked the rolling hills into which the Garonne River doubled back, after suddenly leaving its wide valley to shift brutally into the mountain's side, like a sword thrust sideways, as if seeking a second source. All the small peaks that surrounded the town looked as if they had sprouted up after the mountains and the rivers, in a feverish afterthought, as though the gods had forgotten something when they created this corner of the earth and then decided to add it later on. Cracius loved this spot because it reminded him of the Seven Hills of Rome. In the distance, the Pyrenees radiated their beauty. They were almost too lovely, too regal, and indomitable; he preferred the hills at the foot of the mountain.

Behind him, the city of Lugdunum Convenarum was still dark. The rays of the rising sun hadn't reached it. Still, in places the town was slowly waking up: Cracius could make out the first stirrings. He knew them well: merchants and craftsmen whose early preparations kept him awake when he came in to rest after a night spent carousing. He didn't need to look: he knew the stalls around the forum, the workshops below, further to the North and the houses in the poorer part of town where traditional Gallic dwellings mixed with modern stone houses with curved tiles in the Roman style. Up higher, just below the fortress, standing above the rest of the city was the Roman quarter where the villas and the gardens and orchards were almost as grand as those on the Latium. His back to the city, he admired the high snowy mountain tops standing against the sky at the far end of the valley, sharp as swords. They thrust into the sky, softened only by the round hills at their feet. He felt he could tame the wind and silence the birds. He was invincible and today's magnificent dawn was his only rival for glory. The Romans, after all, were masters of the world, of all that was known from distant Asia to the Celtic shores, from the Nile to the Danube, and he, Cracius, was the strongest, the handsomest and the youngest of all Romans. He thought of Epostorivida: the scent of her skin lingered on his lips and his fingers; he breathed it in again. As he stretched his tired loins he felt he could defy nature itself. He twisted his mouth up to lick the taste of the girl's body on his lips. He remembered her blond mane, looked at the sky and shouted in victory: the sound echoed in the valley and off the surrounding hills, waking a sleeping bird of prey.

Cracius closed his eyes to retain the last remnants of the night's receding pleasures, before heading home. Just a little while ago, as the day was dawning, he had silently left his beautiful victim; now, he would sleep like a tiger returning to its lair. As for the others, the creatures of daylight, let them talk, let them say what they wanted about his escapades. He could hear them all talking behind his back, jealous fathers, envious matrons, the upright and the righteous, who disapproved of him but kept coming to his house to curry favor every day.

Since debauchery hadn't yet become fashionable in the faraway provinces of the Empire, Cracius, whose behavior wouldn't raise an eyebrow in the Latium, here passed for the most scandalous of all the young Roman noblemen of Lugdunum Convenarum. Yet his parties were the most sought after in the city. In his domus, you could forget that Rome, with its pleasures, its luxurious licentiousness and its civilized refinements, was really so far away. His guests enjoyed luxuries such as only the greatest cities in the Empire could offer: an abundance of cooks, young and beautiful servant boys bearing exotic spiced dishes on chiseled silver platters, salted Gallic pork delicacies and fish. Nepos, the impeccable structor who used to work for Quintus Cracius' father in his Palatine villa, oversaw everything. These were not just dinners, simple cenae, but veritable banquets: the wines of Campania and Chios flowed more abundantly than the beer served at other houses; and the evening always ended with dancers and tightrope walkers and no one could figure out how Cracius managed to procure them. Everyone hoped to be granted an invitation but as soon as they had it they felt free to drag his name in the mud. Cracius was aware of this and found it very funny. As one of the great ones of this world, he couldn't care less what the plebs thought or said. Vox populi: what a joke. How could anything so far beneath him ever touch him!

The first rays of the sun touched his hair. On the horse's harness, the shining copper plate of the coat of arms of the Vespasiani danced in the light. The Vespasiani had long been senators of Rome, the eternal city. His grandfather bore that same coat of arms at the battle of Pharsala at Ceasar's side; today, his uncle wore it on his toga at the imperial palace. Cracius Vespasianus was one of the colonists who spread the Empire across the seas and the mountains. He brought with him its ideal of governance and aristocracy. He was the ambassador of a world that had conquered enough and now concentrated all its efforts on spreading Roman culture and civilizing the new territories. Cracius knew that he represented those values. He was Rome in his heart and his soul. He never forgot his rank and the power it carried.

Suddenly he felt tired, sat back in his saddle, rounded his shoulders and breathed in slowly, deeply. His eyes rested on the foothills of the Pyrenees, the wooded landscape cut out against the first line of the snowy mountain tops. Sometimes, like today, this place, this damp province of Aquitaine, where the winters were so much harsher than in the Latium, made him forget the Mediterranean, the nights on the terraces of Ostia and the play of the light on the tall pines of the Capitol. Today he loved the woodsy smells of the earth.

And the wind! It was so windy here: the winds blew from the east and from the west. The Gauls said there were a thousand winds. They made the air thicker, giving it a texture that clung to your face. The wind was like a sixth sense. Even in summer, when the Latium was groaning under the oppressive Roman heat, Lugdunum Convenarum was buffeted by the sea air: it dried all plants and drove the Gauls a bit mad but kept you from feeling caught in a fiery trap as in the Roman basin.

With his arms outstretched he could have embraced the mountains. He would have liked to hold on to this moment, this view. 'I'll ask Plautius Silvanus to paint a monumental fresco in the atrium', he thought. 'But will he be able to paint the wind?' Cracius pressed his legs against his horse, pulling in the reins between his fingers and was going to whip the animal's neck but heard a sudden noise behind his back. Before he could look back, his left shoulder blade was struck very hard and he fell forward. The pain in his back irradiated through his chest. Bent over the horse's neck, he tried to sit up but couldn't. He keeled over and slipped to the side, landing on the cold glistening grass. He'd fallen on his back and the pain was excruciating, as if he'd been hit by a stake, and planted into the ground. He could hardly breathe. His throat emitted a sort of loud gurgling sound. For a few seconds he gave in to the pain, trying to think, to calm down. Something was keeping him impaled on the ground and he was unable to sit up or lie flat. It must be a dagger or a sword; the steel blade was tearing at his flesh and his bones. He had been stabbed and the pain was astonishing. He lifted his head and saw someone standing a few feet away. He lifted an arm, tried to call out. But the other one didn't react. His horse, which had remained still up until then, took a few nervous steps forward dragging Cracius, whose foot was caught in the reins. The wracking tearing pain returned, stronger this time, as the uneven ground tore him apart, as the tall grasses lashed his face, as the scrub and the acorns furrowed into his back while the blade ploughed him apart into the ground. Finally, his foot came loose and his leg thumped to the ground. The horse stopped, Cracius took a cautious breath. He told himself he wasn't dead, not yet. He could make it but he must act fast: that shadow above him stood for death, not help. It was going to come closer to finish him off if he didn't get to his sword. He must stand and fight if he wanted to live. But his sword was tied to the saddle. First he must get up. Once he's standing, things will be better. He turned on his side. But his breathing sounded like a death rattle. He brought both arms together and tried to push his body up, in vain. He'd only managed to push himself up an inch at the most and fell back in an agony of pain. He heard crying and wailing. Was he no longer alone with his aggressor? Had someone come to help him? He must try again to get up; a man who stands on his two legs is not dead; you die when you lie down. He summoned his will, his instinct to survive, the effort made him groan but a force mightier than his own kept him nailed to the earth.

He now lay face up. His killer walked between him and the sun and stood looking at him. Cracius could see that he was crying but couldn't make out his features. Both were still and looked at each other. Cracius wanted to say something but could not. What would he say, anyway? It was too late now. He knew his life was ebbing away. He felt his warm blood wetting the grass and the cold entering his body. And the still, silent shape was watching him die, and didn't help and wasn't going to put an end to his agony.

There was no longer any time to try to understand. He must prepare himself. So he closed his eyes and pictured the Pyrenees: just a while ago they stretched before him and now he was the one lying at their feet. The pain was gone. He was drifting, slowly, quietly. Would he meet the gods?

He heard his horse's hoof striking the ground

II

"What's all this noise about?"

Hadrianus Trevius' voice, loud and commanding, could be heard from his office, and echoed through the atrium where business was conducted and reached the peristyle and the family's private apartments. The screaming and laughter stopped for awhile and then resumed.

"Shouldn't the children be at school at this hour? What's the pedagogue doing?"

A sweet voice was heard and then a slightly deeper one: two boys, the younger eleven, the older fourteen, both answered: "I don't go to school anymore, father; I study at the grammarian's."

"And I study with the rhetor, father."

The magistrate didn't like being interrupted in his work but he wasn't as annoyed as he pretended to be. He got up from his desk and walked to the entrance of the tablinum. He re-adjusted his toga: the children knew what that meant and they ran off. This was a game they played between them and each one knew his role. The happy mischief makers were young but their father, Hadrianus Trevius, was already getting old: he had grown fat under the weight of his responsibilities and weary wisdom had turned his thick hair grey.

"Get your tablets and styles and leave. Your teachers are waiting."

Hadrianus Trevius felt tired. He stretched his limbs caressed by the sun and yawned. This was going to be a busy day and he probably wouldn't be able to take his usual afternoon siesta, or even relax in the bath in his house before tonight's council meeting: there was too much work to be done!

First there was that damned sewer construction project. What made it difficult was that so many houses, workshops and shops had grown in such a disorderly fashion around the forum in the lower city that none of the maps he was supposed to examine and present to the council matched the actual layout. Also, he hated dealing with numbers and regretted not having given the task to Caius Retus, his second magistrate. He would have been just as capable of checking the engineer's report. The engineer and his four slaves, two aquarii and two siphonarii, specialists in supplying water to cities, had come from Tolosa and surveyed the city for three weeks; then they handed in their report and left. The engineers, just like all imperial technocrats, had grand ideas about how other people should spend their money. The 'others' in this case were the honestiores, the leading citizens of Lugdunum Convenarum who would have to agree to finance a sewer system for their town. So it was important to keep an eye on the expenses projected by the engineer.

Lucius and Julius, Hadrianus's two boys, walked by with their pedagogue, a slave their father had brought back from Rome to oversee their studies. He gave both boys a kiss. As they were stepping out into the vestibule, their mother, a statuesque woman, followed by her hairdresser, came from one of the rooms around the atrium. She also asked for a kiss. She was keeping the boys from being on their way, thought Hadrianus, who found women as irritating as any hitch in his schedule; he launched into one of his tirades against the school:

"If these children had their own preceptor and studied at home, I wouldn't mind them being late, but since you insist on forcing our family to bow to the laws of the community I would find it distasteful that they should get to school late." Then, since his outburst had no effect whatsoever and his wife just chuckled, Hadrianus continued, sharply this time: "Stop smothering them in kisses! Lucius is almost old enough to wear the toga and you treat him like a baby."

"Oh my dear, what's wrong with you today?" As she said this she looked up at him and gathered the folds of her dress that had parted to reveal her linen tunic and he glimpsed her full bosom held up by the tight strophium.

"I shouldn't be made to suffer because you spend sleepless nights at your desk. If you spent your nights in a more enter-taining fashion you wouldn't be so cranky."

Claudia realized she shouldn't have uttered those words, as soon as she said them. For a long time now they had agreed not to broach the subject of sex, or rather the absence of sex between them. Claudia didn't complain when he stopped coming to her because she too had wanted their relations to stop. She preferred to sleep alone and Hadrianus busied himself with the affairs of the city.

Claudia was one of the most beautiful women of Lug-dunum Convenarum. Of course she was no longer the young beauty who made men's hearts leap at her sight and made women jealous, but her sensuous hair, her elegance and the heady scents she chose still made her entirely captivating. In fact she was sensuality incarnate and yet had given up the game of seduction long ago: she found joy in being a loving and respected mother to her children. As she was about to apolo-gize, Hadrianus retorted:

"I carry the weight of the city's wellbeing and the interests of the empire on my shoulders. If you need more entertaining nights, why don't you use the services of one of your slaves? I certainly won't mind." A heavy silence followed. The pedagogue pushed the boys towards the door and the servants who were present slipped away. They each walked into one of the rooms off the atrium as on some purposeful errand, pulled the curtain to and stood close by the opening in the hope of catching the rest of the exchange between husband and wife.

But it was in vain because Hadrianus promptly turned back into his office.

The sun had risen, lifting the morning mist, but dew still glistened on the damp ground. Hadrianus wrapped himself in the expensive mohair gausapa he'd bought at Titus's shop on the forum. Titus sold expensive materials and luxury items and kept trying to convince him to wear breeches as some of his Roman colleagues in the council had started to do, but he refused: he felt his position as First Magistrate didn't allow him such carelessness of dress, not even at home. The foolish blabbing slaves would have quickly gossiped all over town spreading the news that their master had taken to dressing in the Gallic fashion. And if the slaves kept quiet then the servants, who were Gauls, would do the talking. As a matter of fact, there had been many occasions when, unbeknownst to them, Hadrianus had used his servants' eagerness to talk. When he wanted to spread a rumor or stop one, all he needed to do was raise his voice slightly within earshot of one his eavesdropping attendants: that same evening the information would start spreading among the population and, three days later, the whole city was in the know. This had often allowed him to issue statements without having to take responsibility for them; he could also crush the opposition without having to fight it openly. He could address the townspeople without having to meet with them and, conversely, find out whatever was being said on the street, without having to go there, as he, in turn, listened to his servants talking amongst themselves.

Eight years had passed since the Emperor had appointed him head of the quattuorvirate in charge of the city and the region. Eight years! He was proud of the peaceful relations he had established between the Gauls and the Romans. It hadn't been easy but he'd decided to include the local aristocracy in the administration of the city and that had been the key to his success: this small region nestled at the foot of the mountains was now successfully romanized.

And yet, when Lugdunum Convenarum had been attached to the new province of Aquitania, Augustus' councilors had tried to dissuade him from turning it into anything more than a fortified town for the strategic control of this newly conquered land. The Emperor, though, had listened to the moderates who advocated collaboration between the victors and the vanquished. He had decided to turn Lugdunum Convenarum into a showcase of the Pax Romana.

The Emperor had not been motivated only by this grand vision: naming Hadrianus to this faraway post meant banishing one of the staunchest defenders of the Republic, a senator who had opposed Augustus' rise to absolute power. Having granted Hadrianus all the powers of a minor regional governor, the Emperor would have good reason to send in the troops, crush the Gauls and dismiss the governor if he failed. If, on the other hand Hadrianus was successful, the Magistrate would have no legitimate reason to request to return to Rome.

Soon after his arrival Hadrianus had made Gedemo Fourth Magistrate of the quatuorvirate governing the city: he was the tribal head of the Convenes who had ruled the region before the Roman invasion, and whose huts had stood where the forum was being built.

Now Hadrianus could be proud of what he had achieved: his power was firmly established and he was a rich man. But he knew how much remained to be done. The city had grown and prospered more than anyone could have predicted. Once the sewer system and the baths were completed, there would be other projects: he was going to make this town into a real Roman city, with government buildings, a theater and schools.

The sweet sound of a harp interrupted Hadrianus's architectural dreams. Staia, his eldest daughter, had started playing. As a girl she had of course not studied beyond the elementary grades; reading and writing were sufficient endowments for a future wife. There was no reason to burden her with knowledge of the world, philosophy, or the intricacies of language and rhetoric. She was being taught music and dance like all girls from good families. Every day, the teacher, Francimo, visited the homes of the rich Roman families and gave them the best instruction in these arts. Francimo was a freed slave who hailed from Tolosa and had put on many shows in that city. Before that he had been a dancer himself for many years in Narbo. It was therefore a source of pride for Hadrianus and Claudia that their daughter was being taught by such a renowned master.

Staia was also learning how to become a good wife, as all young women do, from their mothers, and from her own intuitions and hopes and fears of the day, when, having turned nineteen, she would be married to her betrothed. Ever since it had been settled that she would marry Cracius Vespasianus, her hopes were increasingly tinged with fear. It seemed to her that whatever she thought she knew of what went on between husbands and wives paled before Cracius' reputation: he was said to be handsome, young, rich and a dissolute, hard drinking playboy. The women around Staia tried to reassure her: her beauty, her bountiful curves would conquer and sate the young man; her persistence and feminine wiles would bind him to her and guarantee her happiness. Her attendants, as they massaged her or painted her face, tended to her with knowing smiles and silly giggling. Staia refused to understand them and the experienced slave girls chuckled.

Hadrianus was watching his daughter, in profile against the light, her raven black hair, her straight forehead, and her young downy cheek now resting on the column of the harp: she was looking down and there was such sadness in her face that it was close to melancholy. So young and yet so sad, he thought. Some girls are exactly what men see them as: a sensuous mirror reflecting desire; other girls see only emptiness in that reflection. Such was Staia. Young women like her can never be persuaded that their beauty would set the orient itself ablaze. They still cling to the irrepressible need to retreat into the shadows. And yet, they set fire to those very hearts they wished to hide from.

Hadrianus drew nearer, quietly so as not to disturb her. The contrast between the noisy departure of the boys and the sweet sounds coming from the harp was striking. In the center of the peristyle, he dipped his hands into the small fountain where the rainwater gathered; fresh rose petals had been strewn on the surface and still floated on the clear cool water. He rubbed his hands and his face. The water was still cold from the night and he thought it would wake him up. He let the drops trickle from his forehead down his cheeks and onto his toga and he watched his daughter through the cotton netting that barred the entrance to her room. She hadn't yet seen him but would probably notice him soon and then the charm would be broken. Why deny it? He'd always preferred his daughter to the boys and always thought she had a stronger personality than they did: they were certainly good upstanding lads but they would be less clear sighted and insightful than she was.

Staia realized that she was being observed and turned towards her father. At first she was still lost in the soft reverie of the music, then she smiled gently at her father and he smiled back. Then he turned back into his office once again.

But there wasn't much opportunity to get back to work: the slave standing in the vestibule announced that Lorus Divolus was requesting an interview. Lorus was the overseer of the district and also worked as Hadrianus' personal secretary. A former slave, Lorus had been freed by Hadrianus, and, through hard work and dedication, had risen to the rank of Imperial Civil Servant. People said of him that he was an upright and austere man and these qualities had made him what he was in spite of his humble extraction. But Hadrianus found him sad, pompous and starchy. Lorus Divolus' only interest in life was accounting; nothing excited the man apart from the business of the municipe. He was one of those entirely efficient persons who make themselves absolutely indispensable and therefore absolutely hateful. When Lorus walked in, a sort of chilly formality penetrated the domus like a cold wind.

"Good morning, master. Sorry to bother you."

The obsequious tone of that voice: as if the man was intent on reminding everyone of his lowly status. Hadrianus found him all the more repulsive.

"Good morning, Lorus; what is it that brings you here so early? Couldn't it wait until this afternoon's meeting?"

"Precisely. It's today's meeting I wished to talk to you about." Lorus Divolus paused: he knew that what he had come to say would disturb his master.

"Well?"

"I've been thinking about today's agenda. Maybe you should change it so we don't have to make the appeal for funds quite so soon."

"Nonsense. That's exactly the reason I called the meeting today. Everyone knows it. Everyone's seen the engineer and his men surveying. You'd have to be blind to miss it. And of course, it's been the talk of the town."

"I know, master, but even so, I think it would be best to postpone this call for funds. It's been two years since you solicited the council's generosity for the construction of the baths, and they're still not completed. You risk being severely criticized if you present this new sewer project and again ask for special funds."

"No. We can't put this off. This work is urgent. In any case, sooner or later, it's going to have to be done and the members of the council are going to have to pay."

"It's not just the council members. We already have enough cotton to trample with the work on the baths; we won't be able to see our way through both projects at the same time."

What an unpleasant, vulgar man, thought Hadrianus, put off by the former slave's choice of simile: slaves trampled cotton in urine with their bare feet to prepare it for the dyeing process. Still, he had to admit the man was right: he would be criticized for his haste. He wanted to leave his mark, the mark of Roman civilization on this city, and time, at his age, was running out.

"There's no other way. The population of Lugdunum Convenarum grows with each passing year and I must make sure that the city develops and grows in prestige."

"I understand, master. You are right to look far into the future but you won't always be able to draw funds from both the Roman aristocrats and the merchants. They will tire of it."

"The Gauls will be called upon to contribute in the same way as the Romans. Look at all the stalls and shops that are opening up everywhere: you don't need much foresight to know that the number of contributors will soon double. As for those who refuse to take part in improving the civitas, they will no longer be authorized to sell their wares here."

"When the city's population increases twofold so will the expenses of the municipium. The Elders' contributions will never be enough to cover all the building we are going to have to do in the next ten to twenty years."

"So, what do you propose?"

"The only way is to levy a tax."

Hadrianus laughed bitterly:

"Nothing new there! Even my son Julius who's just turned eleven knows that. But what can I do? Lugdunum Convenarum has not been granted the status of imperial city. Only Augustus could decide that and I don't see why he would do us such a favor. As you know the Emperor does not favor me."

"Well, that's just the point."

"What do you mean?"

"Things can change. It's been eight years since you were banished from Rome and the Senate. You've kept a low profile, you've redeemed yourself. The Emperor may be able to forget that you once opposed him."

Hadrianus shrugged and said with a bitter smile:

"You don't know Augustus."

"Make allegiance to him, Master, flatter him and demonstrate your submission. Don't bring up the matter of the city's status; talk about the Emperor's glory. The Elders' money you are going to spend is not intended to beautify the city and the district, no, let him see that you are spending it for the glory of Rome and Augustus."

Hadrianus stood up. He fiddled nervously with the mother of pearl fibula that held his gausappa, thinking over what Lorus Divolus had just said. He brought out two silver cups, a red ceramic wine pitcher from Graufesenque, and a beaker of fresh water to cut the wine. It was a little early for wine but the overseer wouldn't dare refuse. He was accustomed to Hadrianus' very Roman habit of drinking a cup of wine regularly throughout the day, as his doctors had prescribed. He also accepted the dried apricots his master offered him.

"From Armenia", said Hadrianus absentmindedly, as if they were some fruit from the garden.

The First Magistrate started pacing up and down the room, eyes to the floor, popping pieces of fruit into his mouth one after the other and chewing nervously. Lorus waited for his master to resume the exchange.

"What are you thinking of exactly? I can't very well invite Augustus here to show him my plans for the city or have him taste the pure waters of the Pyrenees and admire Gallic craftsmanship!"

"Since you can't bring Augustus here himself, bring his likeness."

"What do you mean, his likeness? What kind of riddle is this? You're talking like an augur."

"Bring the name and the glory of the Emperor to the city. Make Lugdunum Convenarum into the very incarnation of Rome's power in Gaul."

"These are just words. I still don't see what could move Augustus to change his mind about me."

Hadrianus gulped down the last of the apricots and took a sip of wine.

"Augustus has just crushed the Cantabri and the Astures of Hispania, he's suppressed any desire for rebellion among the Aquitanians and he's created the three provinces of Gaul. In the space of a few years, he's spread Rome's power all the way to Britannia."

"He has, I know that. But how does that concern our city?"

"Well, Lugdunum Convenarum is now at the epicenter of Augustus's conquests; it lies at the crossroads of Hispania, the new province of Aquitania and the Narbonensis. It can become the key to the central Pyrenees. The mountains have mineral ore; the valleys are rich in fertile land; the Garonne runs close by the civitas: commerce can only grow. Let us build a Roman city, let us give it all the trappings of civilization. Then, Lugdunum Convenarum will be a showcase for Augustus' achievements. He himself doesn't know it yet: you are the one who will make him see the strategic and political importance of the city. That is how you will convince him that we deserve the status of imperial city. And by then, of course, you will have become First Magistrate of one of the richest regions of Aquitania, as rich as Tolosa."

There was a long silence. Lorus let the honey of his words distill itself in his master's mind.

Hadrianus took another sip of wine.

He had always considered his posting to Lugdunum Convenarum as a form of political exile. During the first few months, he had tasted the full bitterness of exile: he was an outcast, a fallen man. Then as time blunted the pain and resignation took over, he found consolation in the idea that maybe he could enjoy being a great man in a small place. News of his friends who like him had opposed Augustus's growing power and the Senate's subjection, helped to convince him that he'd been lucky. They had not left Rome and their sentences had been swift and final.

Still, he had never thought of this small Gallic region as a springboard for his ambitions.

And now, the city overseer, a former slave, had shown him what should have been obvious all along. He turned round suddenly and bursting with sudden enthusiasm, almost shouted:

"I've got an idea. We shall build a victory monument to Augustus. A gigantic trophy, twice as tall as the one erected in Urculu for Agrippa and Messala... larger even than the one that was built to commemorate Pompey's victory over Sertorius, in Pernissass. I'll have it cut and carved by sculptors from the Latium: our Gauls can only work the wood from their forests. On the other hand, the white marble from the Pyrenees is magnificent and its pure color can be found nowhere else in the world; we'll have it hauled over here from Passus Lupi. We'll pay for the carting ourselves. And, this time, the Gauls will also be paying: it will be their gift to the Emperor. But of course, Augustus must not be allowed to forget that I'm the one initiating all this."

And so Lorus Divolus approved an idea he himself had suggested, and he did so silently, as should a former slave, who accepted reality as it was. But it added fuel to the long simmering resentment, burning inside him. It was like the oil that kept the lamp slowly but steadily burning in his black heart. Such a tiny flickering flame of revenge would probably never set fire to anything but it stubbornly refused to die.

Hadrianus, rapt in his own dream, filled another cup for Lorus and himself. The excitement made him giddy. Drinking the wine without any water now, he felt it had opened his eyes and, gazing into it he could see the truth finally unveiled. Spurred on by the drink, he felt inspired to new heights of fancy; he'd completely forgotten that the idea had come from Lorus. It was his initiative now, his monument, his vision:

"Then, we'll rename the city, we'll call it Lugdunum Convenarum Augustunum. Never before has such an honor been bestowed upon the Emperor in the provinces, and with such zeal. Augustus wishes to be venerated like a demigod by the people, both in Rome and in the most remote provinces; he wants his palace on top of the Palatine hill to be the replica of Jupiter's celestial throne. Well, we will let him slake his thirst for glory. Augustus the god will be served, if that is the way to his heart."

Lorus Divolus bowed his head and listened. He was silently thinking, thinking ahead, planning, projecting, counting. There was enough time, he would find the means, somehow, to make apparent his role as initiator of this project, and to garner at least some small advantage, some degree of recognition for himself. He knew that the magistrates of the Quattuorvirate depended on him, the freed slave: only he had the skills to manage and run such an operation. And if this tribute to

Augustus did mark a turning point in the city's history and set a new beginning for Hadrianus' career, why shouldn't he too, reap some benefit? He and his family might be granted Roman citizenship! After all, he played a far more pivotal role in the running of the city than many of the aristocrats. They acknowledged his competence and his zeal; yet they begrudged him the title of Roman citizen!

Hadrianus reclined on the couch he had placed in his office since he sometimes took his meals there. Lorus was standing. In the magistrate's mind, cold reason and calculation had now overcome euphoria. In the past, he had quarreled more than once with the Emperor in the Senate and he knew that Augustus would not take the bait so easily: it was going to take more than a monument and a few ceremonies in honor of Caesar's family gods for him to regain the emperor's favor.

"How do you think I should behave in order to win over the emperor the way you just did with me?"

This was a moment to savor for Lorus. Once again, Hadrianus was appealing to him, bowing to his wisdom.

"If you wish to convince a man who is above you to act as you have designed, you must convince him that the idea was his own."

Hadrianus froze, stunned and outraged at such gall. He searched Lorus' eyes: maybe he'd been wrong to allow the man to become so deeply immersed into his affairs.

In the silence that ensued, the various sounds of the household took over again. An odor of garum floated up from the kitchen. Asinius had probably just received a shipment and was busy pouring the precious condiment into serving bowls.

Hadrianus returned to his desk, sat down and took up the tablets he'd been working on when Lorus came in:

"If there's nothing more, you may leave, Lorus." His tone was curt; Lorus bowed slightly and took his leave.

"Good day, master. Until tonight at the Curia."

"Yes, till tonight."

Lorus withdrew, and, as he let the curtain fall, one could hear the clear notes of Staia's harp. They echoed again through the peristyle, at the back of the house. But the sweet melody was not enough to lure Hadrianus from his thoughts: that overseer of his was too clever by half. He would have to be much more wary of a man of his ilk, a freed slave who believed he could think for his master.

III

Harero was running so fast he could hardly breathe. Stones cut his feet, he'd left his flock up there, his stick got caught in a bush, and he didn't even try to retrieve it, he didn't think, he ran, and ran, and wouldn't look back.

The sweat running down his face mixed with tears and spittle. A mix of fluids and of fears. Harero feared what he was running away from, but he also feared what he was running to. He felt lost: he had seen evil, how could he escape from it now?

He'd never run so fast for so long. The dead man's image was pursuing him and urging him down the mountain at breakneck speed.

There's a time and a place for dying or for looking at death, there are times when it's expected. But when you're ten years old, on a peaceful afternoon, up in the pasture, in the grass and among the flowers, the time is not right.

Harero had been surprised by time, overwhelmed by it. The gods had put him through a test he was too young to be subjected to. He wished he hadn't seen what his eyes had seen, but it was too late. He'd seen that face, those large open eyes staring up at the sky, staring into nothingness, widened by incomprehension, and that half opened mouth, as if death had stifled a cry.

What could he do? From now on he would have to live with that sight.

These eyes, that mouth. He had recognized the rich Roman. He had recognized his horse from afar, before he'd seen him lying there, unconscious, a few paces away. He had seen his body, and he had come closer. He knew what to expect. Still, he had called out, to wake the man lying there. In vain. He had come even closer and called again. There wasn't a sound, only the wind blowing and the ewes bleating and his own breathing, loud in his ears and his own quivering voice pleading 'don't let him be dead, just asleep; I'm going to wake him up, he's going to be startled, and he'll scold me but that's all.'

These eyes, that mouth.

Could that mouth have something to say? Could it say something? The young goatherd was too scared to hear it. It didn't concern him. He didn't want to know! All he wanted was to get away as fast as possible and never return, and forget what he had seen. Cracius was dead. Let his soul go wherever it might!

"I approve the measures being proposed by the quattuor-virate. The region must be allowed to enjoy all the comforts and the benefits of Roman civilization…"

Vettius Gracilis had just started speaking. Calidius Iassus, the Third Magistrate, sat down after his presentation of the feeder canal and sewer project. Hadrianus signaled his approval with a slight nod in his direction: there was nothing to add or change to what had been said and that was exactly as it should be. He did not want to take part in the debate until the very last moment, when he could act as judge and not as prosecutor. The councilors kept quiet for the moment but Hadrianus knew from long practice that the discussion would be raucous as it always was when the issue involved committing large sums of money. He enjoyed the power, however small, that his accession to the post of First Magistrate of Lugdunum Converanum gave him. In Rome, when he was a senator, he had worked for the good of the people, he'd spoken in their name. But here, far from Rome, he had to admit having strayed far from his republican ideals. Augustus had now become his model for wielding power. To think that for so long he had fought Augustus' conception of autocratic power in the name of those ideals!

Vettius Gracilis stood up as Balbius Iassus sat down: the curia resembled a game of ninepins going up and down or some ridiculous troupe of dancers. Vettius was at the head of the guild of Roman merchants.

"Even before this council had been created, and before most of us had arrived in Lugdunum Convenarum, the first settlers of the city agreed to finance the construction of the forum. Later, we were again willing to support, with our own funds, the construction of a port on the river Garonne because we were convinced that the city and the whole region would eventually play an important role in the wealth of the empire. Later still, Hadrianus asked for baths, because of their importance in our social life. That, once again, meant very important outlays for us. Today, as the benefits of our trade are only beginning to offset all these expenditures, the baths are still not completed. And now, again, the Quattuorvirate is appealing to our generosity."

Vettius was a good businessman but he was also a very good orator. He knew how to modulate his voice, pitching his tone between refusal and goodwill. The councilors showed their support or their disagreement with discreet nods or even a few reticent interjections. Everyone was still very restrained. Hadrianus, as they all knew, hated disorderly council meetings, just as he had during his years in the Senate: in his eyes disorder was just as unbecoming in an empire as it had been during the republic.

Outside, the public who were sitting on the steps leading up to the curia or standing in the square in front of the building were hoping to catch the first volley. Romans and Gauls had assembled in the forum, as they always did when spring arrived, to meet neighbors and friends. They listened to the debates or lingered in the afternoon sun. They watched as the plumes of smoke rising from the chimneys were blown by the wind toward the pastures where they mingled with the mist lifting from the meadows. From time to time, they would send someone off to glean some snatches of the debate, or report some wisecrack. "So, what did Hadrianus say?", "What did Gedemo answer Dracus?", "How did Festus react to Francimo's attack?" The messenger would report back and he would be greeted with laughter or outrage, and then everyone would go back to their leisurely business. Some families sat down in the grass and shared millet cakes.

Hadrianus and his three colleagues of the Quattuorvirate sat in the center of the great hall of the curia. Behind them stood Lorus, invisible but, at the same time, omnipresent. To the magistrates' right sat the Roman councilors; they faced their Gallic counterparts who were sitting to the left of the magistrates. Hadrianus had decided that it would be so as soon as he had taken over: the civitas would be governed jointly and the future of the Roman people and of the Gallic people would thus be linked.

The hall was painted with frescoes commissioned by Hadrianus, such as wouldn't have been out of place in Rome. Everything had been modeled on the Roman Curia: the steps that led up to the council hall, the huge open porch that allowed the people to witness the debates, the seating plan of the magistrates and the councilors, down even to the stucco bas-relief, an exact replica of the one adorning the walls of the Roman Senate house, that now graced the otherwise austere building.

Harero, the young goatherd, had finally stopped running. He had burst into the thatched wood hut where his family huddled, seeking the safety of their arms. Now, the terrible news he brought had begun on its own course, out the door and then from one hut to the next inside the Gallic hamlet, and then, like sylphs, like fire-spirits, had leapt on toward the city.

The elder Harero, the shepherd, had turned to his wife and said:

"Not a word of this to anyone. Cracius is a Roman. We have nothing to do with this."

His wife had been combing wool when her son rushed in screaming; she nodded her assent but her hands did not take up their work. It was no use. In the village, all activity had stopped and everyone had gathered to hear of the event. The news was already making the rounds, house to house, field to neighboring field, wood to neighboring wood: "Cracius is dead, Cracius is dead. He's up there, on the peak, the one with the great oak tree; he's lying in the grass; it's him, there's no doubt, it's his horse; little Harero, Harero the shepherd's son, recognized him."

Vettius Gracilis was still talking. Hadrianus could have recited every word of his speech, he could have given it himself: "It isn't right that only the Romans should be asked to contribute; why shouldn't the Gallic tradesmen and craftsmen shoulder some of the cost: they profit from all the progress being made and yet, they don't pay..." Hadrianus knew that these words were certain to rouse the Gauls' indignation: they would counter that they had never asked for anything, that they had lived very well, thank you, before the Romans colonized the land of the Convenes. He would have to pander to one group while reassuring the other; but their opposition suited him well for the time being because it allowed him to govern by promising everything to one party and the opposite to the other party.

So now, of course, Francimo, Gedemo's right hand man and probably a future magistrate of the civitas, rose up to speak. He faced Vettius and prepared to answer him in the name of the Gauls. Everything opposed the two men: their height, the color of their hair, their manner of speaking. Francimo was a Celt who still spoke a halting Latin; he was taller and more light skinned than Vettius Gracilis whose darker complexion and well groomed brown hair signaled his Mediterranean origins. Only their clothes were not so dissimilar: both dressed in a half Roman half Celtic fashion.

Francimo was known to be blunt. On both sides of the hall councilors sat up and pricked their ears.

"The Gauls will be honored to take part in the city's development … when they have the honor of being Roman citizens. For the moment, we don't see why we should be willing to contribute to the prosperity of an empire that grants us no rights and offers us no recognition."

The game of ninepins went on: one man stood up, and another sat down. Francimo and Vettius knew how to play the game together.

"You know very well that, sooner or later, as was the case in the Narbonensis, you will obtain the citizenship that Rome so generously grants, among the other advantages of civilization, to all vanquished barbarian peoples." His words and his tone had been calculated to offend and provoked the expected commotion among the Convenes. But Vettius Gracilis wasn't finished:

"Such is Augustus's will but you must also demonstrate your own goodwill. You shall be granted this privilege as soon as you demonstrate a real desire to participate in the destiny of the civitas. The Roman merchants are sick and tired of being systematically taxed to bring about improvements which all the Convenes will enjoy without ever having contributed to any part of the financial burden."

These words went beyond simple provocation and the public outside instinctively drew nearer. Those who had been hoping for some scandal or some clash, sensed that now something serious was brewing. Hadrianus felt it was time for him to intervene. He got up: that was enough to silence the councilors and put an end to the commotion among the public. He opened his arms in an imposing gesture of peace; the setting sun laid golden rays on his white toga while the purple edge of the cloth hinted at evening. He stood like a man walking out of the light and stepping into darkness; he noticed it and was quite proud of the effect this was having on the audience.

"That the Roman corporations should feel resentful at the injustice is all too understandable but Francimo's point of view is not without merit. Still, I would like to remind you that the greatest sacrifices up to now have not been made by the merchants but by the Roman aristocracy and most notably, by the Vespasiani. I wouldn't want to underestimate the part your corporation has played, Vettius, but it's far less than that of the few knightly families of our city, and it is out of any proportion to the benefits that you have enjoyed."

Vetttius wasn't going to be impressed by histrionics and golden togas. The First Magistrate's words were intended to remind him that in this caste system, every man was a plebeian to his superiors. He didn't dispute the sums alluded to nor did he challenge the lesson in humility. He counterattacked shamelessly by going at the unassailable star of Lugdunum Convenarum's aristocracy:

"The Vespasiani..."

Vettius paused for a few heavy seconds; everyone was holding their breath.

"... who are conspicuous by their absence from any meeting of the council. Maybe that is an indication of how concerned they are for the welfare of our city."

Not a sound could be heard after that. The two men faced each other, alone.

"The Vespasiani have given more to the city than any of you in this hall; you cannot say that they are indifferent to the fate of Lugdunum Convenarum, and you would be wrong to come to hasty judgments as to the manner in which they conduct their business and acquit themselves of their obligations."

Vettius Gracilis laughed a little too loud. The other delegates of the Roman corporations were careful not to imitate him; they feared possible retribution should this taboo be broken. It wasn't done to poke fun at the mighty of this world and Vettius was going too far. They admired his temerity but didn't want to be associated with it. Bravely, Vettius continued:

"Cracius Vespasianus is mostly known for ..."

Everyone knew what he meant. They wanted him to finish the sentence and at the same time they feared that he would. They were eager to hear the words; they relished the prospect of seeing Hadrianus, for once, with his back to the wall, forced to reply. The entire council, the public itself were tense with anticipation. Each one felt his stomach tighten, as if he too were on the verge of speaking the words, just like Vettius. Some narrowed their eyes in fear and anticipation: let him say it, they thought, and let us witness a rare moment of lèse-majesty; don't say it because Hadrianus's wrath will be indiscriminate.

"...for the care with which he fulfills his obligations toward his fellow libertines and for the way he conducts his nocturnal affairs."

Vettius Gracilis, the lowly tradesman had defied the aristocracy. He had just said what everyone whispered on the street but never dared say out loud, and certainly never in the council chamber.

Outside, people were flocking to the square and gathering from all around the forum. But what attracted them was not the debate; there was another piece of news that was coming from the outside and was making its way through the crowd. It was being passed on from man to woman, young to old, from Roman to Gaul, all the way up to the curia. As the terrible news grew nearer, the crowd wavered and then parted to let the bearer of the news come through: she was Proneotore, the woman from the hamlet beyond the blue peak. She was saying that Cracius was up there, lying in the grass.

"Who's up there?"

"Cracius Vespasianus. They saw his horse, his white horse."

"Cracius' horse. He's up there, dead."

"The horse?"

"No. Cracius Vespasianus himself."

"The horse stayed, right next to him. He didn't move. Cracius loved that horse and now the horse has returned his love. It stayed there, next to its dead master lying in the grass."

"Who died?"

"Cracius."

"He's dead. Dead. There's blood, they say, a lot of blood."

"The people of the hamlet, they're scared; they don't dare go up there. Little Harero, the son of Harero the shepherd, he found him."

"Who's that? Who found him?"

"The shepherd Harero, he found Cracius. Someone has to inform the garrison; he has to be brought back, he can't be left there like that."

At first, Hadrianus' face flushed with fury, but then it turned pallid, and he stared at him with cold, threatening rage.

Vettius was in much greater danger now than if Hadrianus had immediately flown into a rage. The merchant was taking the measure of his audacity and had begun to lose his proud bearing. He sat down, hunched over on his seat, gathered his tunic and wiped his brow. No one dared look at him. Those who sat next to him started moving away.

"You forget that you are speaking about my future son in law, Vettius Gracilis…"

His voice was full of barely veiled menace.

"… and you forget as well that Cracius's second name, Octavus, was given him in honor of his aunt Apronia's cousin, our Emperor, Augustus."

A tremor ran through the crowd but it came from the public outside, not from the councilors' benches. It rumbled through the crowd, shook the first benches in the hall, and then burst forth into the center of the hall. A great cry, sharp and clear, resonated in the curia, interrupting Hadrianus. Proneotore, out of breath, disheveled, sweat pouring down her face, was suddenly shouting:

"Cracius is dead! Cracius Vespasianus is dead!"

IV

Darkness had already fallen when the soldiers reached the bare peak crowned by the majestic old oak tree. Valerius Musa's men carried torches to search the area hoping to find even the smallest trace, the faintest prints of an animal, something that could explain how Cracius had fallen from his horse. Hadrianus himself was overseeing the search. He had dismissed the council members who had accompanied him here, had dispatched the tragic news to Quintus Vespasianus Maximus, Cracius's father, and posted guards all around the hills to prevent anyone going up. Valerius was stooped over the body. He turned it over very carefully and saw the knife planted between the young man's shoulder blades. Ants had started crawling into the open wound. A sharp smell drifted up when the Centurion lifted the right shoulder: the blood had congealed into a syrupy black mass mixed with dirt and clumps of grass.

Hadrianus walked over to the Centurion and Valerius stood at attention. He felt a kind of awkward distress: he knew Cracius was to marry Staia, Hadrianus's daughter.

"I'm very sorry, Hadrianus. Your daughter will be terribly affected."

Hadrianus glanced at the body and, without replying to Valerius, declared:

"Cracius died from an accidental fall."

This wasn't an explanation: it sounded more like an order.

Valerius didn't know what to make of it. He didn't understand.

"For now, this is the official version. Continue to search for clues and keep this place off limits. I'm going to have the men bring up a carriage."

Valerius was dumbfounded; he couldn't help expecting an explanation but there wasn't going to be any.

"What about the dagger in Cracius's back?"

"No one, apart from you and your men, has seen it or knows about it. Make sure that they keep quiet, as I know you will."

He spoke in the curt haughty tone of one dealing with his inferiors. Valerius was no fool: Hadrianus might have looked like a big likeable cat, but he could quickly turn into a tiger with very sharp claws.

"But what about the blood, all this blood in the grass? Cracius bled to death; surely, everyone will have seen it."

"Everyone saw some blood but that's not surprising since Cracius, when he fell, was impaled on that sharp piece of wood that you and your men, in the dark, mistook for the handle of a dagger."

Hadrianus stooped to pick up a broken branch lying in the grass, rubbed it into the puddle of blood near the corpse and handed the bloodied stick to Valerius:

"When your men have taken Cracius away, you will place this where the body was found."

Valerius Musa turned to his men; they were looking away. The reasons behind this charade escaped them, but, after all, to each his own worries. So, they had turned their backs and they went on with their search but without much conviction.

"Cracius fell off his horse, was impaled on this dead branch and the foot of the oak and bled to death. If your men, Valerius, say anything different, if there's the smallest rumor that things didn't happen the way I just described, you will be held responsible. And now, tell your men to take him away and carry him home."

This time, there could be no doubt. Valerius knew he wasn't going to be given an explanation as to why Hadrianus felt compelled to pretend the murder was an accident. That he could have been involved himself or that he could have wanted to protect a murderer was unthinkable. Valerius had always thought of Hadrianus as a fairly honest man. In any case, this was not the place or the time to ask any such questions.

He readjusted his helmet and with a weary gesture, called back his men who were still pretending to look for the traces of a snake or a wild boar.

"Your orders will be carried out."

A short time later, Quintus Vespasianus, Cracius's father, arrived. He got off his horse and threw himself on his son's body. Hadrianus stood back, unable to say a word. The pity he felt for Quintus was mixed with his own sorrow. What could words convey, in such instances? He simply moved up to his friend, knelt beside him and placed his hand on his shoulder. Quintus didn't utter a single word, he didn't cry. He held his son tightly, so tightly he would have hurt him had he been alive. Then he deposited him carefully on the ground and, without turning to Hadrianus, asked:

"What happened?"

"We think he fell from his horse."

"Cracius? Fall from his horse?"

"The horse may have been scared by something and reared up."

"But why all this blood?"

"Most probably Cracius fell on his back and onto this branch. It must have planted itself in his back and then…"

Quintus looked at the branch and at the pool of blood, and again at his son. He got up, covered his mouth with his fist to stifle a moan, and before it might happen again, caught the reins of Cracius' horse and got back on his own.

"Bring my son back to our house, please, Hadrianus."

He dug his heels into the horse's sides. The horse broke into a full gallop, followed by Cracius' mount. Valerius watched them both disappear. Never again would he look Quintus in the eyes; being a party to this lie made him feel ashamed.

The First Magistrate would have preferred that the body be brought home discreetly, but almost everyone was there: Romans, Gauls, slaves and citizens, tradesmen, craftsmen, friends of the nobility, they all waited for Hadrianus and Musa to bring down the young man's body so that they could accompany it across the fields, into the lower city, and up to the family's domus.

To ensure secrecy and to prevent too many soldiers coming up to the spot where Cracius had been lying, Hadrianus had asked the five legionaries to bring down the body immediately. A carriage could not make it up there, the climb was too steep and the path too difficult; the men had to transport him on a stretcher, by hand. They took turns carrying Cracius who had been a strapping fellow at the peak of his form and probably weighed no less than two hundred pounds, not counting his harness and his sword. The small escort started on the stony path that little Harero had run down earlier that afternoon. One soldier lit the way with a torch, two more did the carrying, the fourth one held another torch to guide Hadrianus' steps and together, Valerius Musa and the fifth legionary made up the rear. The men carrying the body struggled to keep it steady when their caligae hit the larger rocks on the way. With every jolt they expected to hear Cracius moan, as if his wide open eyes could still see and his open mouth could speak. Hadrianus attempted to hide Cracius' face but his toga was covered with blood. Valerius offered his own red centurion's toga.

The distance between the peak and the city was at least two miles and the legionaries were already tired and drenched in sweat when they reached the bottom. Once there, Hadrianus ordered that all those who wanted to help or attempted to touch the body as it passed be held back.

Soon after, they reached the carriage and the legionaries could unburden themselves.

The number of people joining the procession grew as they were approaching the city. All were somber and silent. There were no tears, no wailing. Cracius hadn't been a popular man in the civitas. The people hadn't gathered out of sympathy for the deceased. But they all had a feeling that this death did not bode well for them. They probably felt compassion for themselves. They passed along and spread the words that Hadrianus said as he passed in front of them: there had been an accident, he fell off his horse, a mortal fall. It was the first violent death in Lugdunum Convenarum, the first premature death of a Roman aristocrat and everyone felt bewildered and anxious, as if it were a bad omen, a sign sent to the city by the gods, warning of dark times ahead or maybe even worse, a sign of their wrath against the city. Some Convene farmers covered their faces as they went by to avoid looking at the dead man. The Gauls believed that looking into a dead man's face brought bad luck. Hadrianus overheard their fearful warnings and he felt uneasy. He didn't like other people's fear: it was unsettling to him and he felt infected by it. The silent march through the orchards on the outskirts of the city, the light from the torches projecting the silhouettes of the trees like furrows on the blue, moonlit ground, made his blood run cold. The only sounds to be heard were the crowd's footsteps, the groaning of the carriage wheels and the muttered words of the mourners. It seemed to him this march would never end. He yearned with all his heart to get away from these shadows, these ghosts lying across the way; he wanted to deliver the body at Cracius' house, pay his respects to the family, and, finally, go home and throw himself on his knees at the altar to his family gods and find solace in prayer.

Hadrianus was seized by a terrible fear, the worst kind: fear of the unknown. He himself had nothing to do with Cracius' death, of course, but he'd lied to his friend Quintus. Cracius was to become his son in law, and now he was hiding the truth about his death. And this wasn't the end of it; he was going to have to lie again, this time to his own daughter. It seemed to him that all these people lined up on the side of the road were there to judge and blame him. This had not been a natural death. Order would have to be restored; the city would have to pay for this crime and, since he was First Magistrate, he would be the one singled out for punishment by the Gods: they would surely not allow this lie to go unpunished. He must send for Saturnina immediately. Apart from prayer it was the best thing he could do. Saturnina was a sorceress but also something of an augur. She possessed unguents that purified men's bodies and souls. He would pay her, dearly, to consult the gods, all night if need be, until he was completely reassured.

V

The sorrow in Cracius Vespasianus' house was so heavy that Hadrianus could have touched it; it was too close to him: it might infect him; it was like a bog and he could be sucked into it. An awful weight pressed down on his lungs, as if he should hold his breath and try not to inhale the foul air of this house. Had he not been restrained by the laws of civility, he would have stopped his ears against the cries of grief of Quintus' wife. She was taken to her apartments; the servants had to tear her away from her son's body, while the slaves were preparing a soothing potion to numb her pain. Her wailing terrified Hadrianus; it would cast an evil spell on all who heard her. The Vespasiani's slaves had taken the body as soon as it entered the door. Hadrianus was received by Quintus Vespasianus Maximus. Valerius Musa and his legionaries stayed back, standing at attention: their military stiffness shielded them from embarrassment. Hadrianus embraced Lucilla, Cracius' sister and again offered Quintus his condolences. Quintus thanked him but seemed to think there should be no further outpourings of grief. He had Cracius' body laid out in front of the altar to the family gods, the lararium, and sent everyone back to their rooms except the doctor. The peristyle was quiet again. The crying and the wailing had receded into Apronia's apartment. There a bevy of slaves busied themselves, running to the kitchen and bringing back boiling water for the herbal infusions. Others had gone out armed with scythes and saws to gather branches of fir to purify the family's domus.

Valerius Musa stood back a little distance from the honestiores. Quintus was a large man, very imposing because of his height and the sense of raw power that emanated from him. He was the only person Hadrianus really feared in Lugdunum Convenarum. He possessed huge estates both in Italy and in the provinces. His family was one of the richest in Rome. He spent most of his time traveling from the capital to his estates in the Narbonensis and now in Aquitania where he had decided to invest. The reason he had come here was to increase his wealth but also to find some occupation for his son whose life of debauchery in Rome had to come to an end. Quintus had hoped that, away from his friends, Cracius would change and learn to appreciate the virtues of work but the young man seemed to have brought his Roman habits with him here and he had become a source of scandal rather than pride for his father; his behavior could even, in the long run, have become a liability for Quintus's expansionist projects in Aquitania.

Quintus called out his son's name, several times, according to custom, to make certain he was dead. Then, as he watched, the family clinicus started examining Cracius' body. He concentrated on the wound between the shoulder blades, measured it and inserted a scalpel deep into it. Then he turned to his master. They spoke in a low voice: Quintus' doctor had quickly determined that Cracius hadn't died from a fall, but that he'd been murdered. Hadrianus' attempt to hide the fact, whatever its motivations, had failed; the truth would have to come out. There would be an investigation.

Valerius witnessed the scene and saw the embarrassment on Hadrianus' face. How could he ever have thought, even for a moment, that he could fool Quintus and his doctor?

Quintus' face had become distorted, as if pulled down by a heavy grey veil. Grief struck him with full force and he almost gave in. Valerius thought he could see tears on his face, a face he'd always known to be impenetrable.

He now turned to Hadrianus who was becoming increasingly uneasy. Very quickly, the lines of sorrow receded on Quintus' face, as if the cloud that had momentarily hidden his hard, strong features had passed. He looked straight into the Magistrate's eyes. No more lies; he wanted to know; he wanted to understand, at this very moment:

"My son was stabbed, Hadrianus. Did you know it?"

"Your doctor says so."

"Yes, and he's a very good doctor. This thing about the branch on which Cracius supposedly impaled himself doesn't hold water. What really happened, Hadrianus?"

"Honestly, I don't know. I would tell you if I knew something."

There were so many questions to ask; Quintus didn't know where to begin.

"The doctor says Cracius was stabbed by a dagger or a small sword. Was anything found up there? Did the search bear any fruit, Valerius?"

Quintus was looking over the Magistrate's shoulder and called to the centurion still standing outside. Valerius walked to the threshold of the peristyle but Hadrianus didn't step aside; instead, he answered in his place:

"No Quintus, we haven't found anything conclusive yet."

But Quintus wasn't going to let him interfere between him and the centurion; he walked up to Valerius and asked the question again:

"Have your men found anything?"

Valerius felt trapped. He didn't know which of the two dangers he faced was worse. His men, standing behind him, were hoping not to be questioned. Valerius looked to

Hadrianus for a clue. Quintus was fast losing patience at the centurion's hesitant silence. He wasn't a man of good will and his son had died that night. He could kill if someone opposed him. He turned to Hadrianus and then to Valerius again, looking back and forth at the two of them.

"What's going on here? Valerius, what are you hiding?"

"I'm a legionary, Quintus, and I follow the orders of the First Magistrate of the city; I'm not obliged to answer you if he will not allow it."

"What does this mean? Hadrianus, this is my son, your future son in law. You can't... You must tell me the truth. What happened?"

Hadrianus now had no choice. From the folds of his toga he pulled out the dagger rolled inside a cotton scarf.

Quintus took the cotton doll in one hand and unfolded it with the other. When he finally saw the very long handle and the short blade, he recognized the Gauls' characteristic weapon.

"I didn't want to tell you before I investigated. I..."

Hadrianus didn't know what to say; in any case, Quintus wasn't listening. At first, his whole body seemed to go limp, like the body of his son that morning on the horse's neck, but he didn't fall to the ground; instead, he immediately straightened up. His anger was palpable. He was so close that Hadrianus could feel it and, instinctively, he took a step back. Quintus now stood with his back to Valerius who saw the muscles in his back tighten through the fine cloth of his toga. The centurion motioned to his men to be ready to intervene if he became violent.

"And you intended to investigate how? Without letting on about the knife?"

"No, of course not but I figured there was no need to create an incident between the Gauls and the Romans before we know more."

"You want to avoid an uprising, is that it? My son was murdered, but the only thing that matters to you is that the streets of Lugdunum Convenarum remain quiet."

"You know how much I loved Cracius; he was like a son to me…"

"And still, you place your good relations with the Gauls first."

"I understand your anger, Quintus, but I promise you: in order to find Cracius' murderer, in order to conduct the investigation, we need the city to be quiet; the investigation must be discreet."

"What I'm convinced of is this: if my doctor hadn't found out that the wound was caused by a blade there would never have been an investigation. Your only goal is to remain as head of the council and to avoid any turmoil because of this incident."

Hadrianus had been caught out; Quintus was right. Still, he parried immediately:

"Quintus, please! We have been friends long enough for you not to doubt my good faith. We don't want conflict in the civitas. My only wish is to find out the truth, just like you, but discreetly. I was afraid of your reaction; I can't let you wage war because of this one clue. This dagger could very well have been stolen from a Convene and used to kill your son in order to incriminate the Gauls."

"We have been friends for many years, it's true; but it's also true that you have turned into a friend of the Convenes. I have always disapproved of the way you treat them, but I don't care whether my son's assassin is a Gaul or a Roman. What I want is for him to be found and I want to see him drawn and quartered on the forum: that's all. Cracius would have been twenty five this summer; Valerius has twenty five days to find the murderer. After that, I'll be the one to wage war, as you say, and I won't take any prisoners, I promise you."

VI

Valerius Musa poured himself a bowl of herbed wine. He added a little honey and warm water: Spring had started but it was still cool in the evenings. He always drank wine in a bowl. The five decurions who shared what used to be the officers' quarters with him came over. One of them always made fun of Valerius' strange habit: everyone drank wine from a cup nowadays. But on that night no one made fun. That night, they watched him prepare the wine and waited for him to start talking.

When he had returned to the camp, the decurions had been playing a game of dice, but clearly, they had been waiting for him. The news of Cracius' death had quickly made the rounds in the city and finally reached the fort where the legionaries lived. The fort, in those days, wasn't as tightly sealed off from the town as it had been. The wooden palisades, the embankments and the ditches were the only remnants from the time when Lugdunum Convenarum served as a fallback position for Pompey's armies, and there were only a few Gallic huts a little further down the hill. There had been a whole legion here, thousands of men, captains and even a general, Pompey himself. Nowadays, Valerius Musa was the highest ranking officer;

he was in charge of a single maniple that had been detached from a cohort in Tolosa. The fort was the only remaining sign of Augustus' wars against the Gauls.

The officers' quarters consisted of an office, a changing room and three bedrooms. Valerius had his own room but his men came and went, without any regard for the centurion's privacy, until nighttime. Valerius would never have tolerated such familiarity in a larger garrison, but in this small outpost, he took no offense. He'd known most of these men, decurions and legionaries, for years. Some had even fought in the same campaigns with him. Valerius was an old soldier now; after twenty years of service, after marching through all the Roman provinces his pack on his back, his heavy helmet on his head and his pilum on his shoulder, after fighting the German barbarians, the Bretons and finally the Aquitanians, he no longer wished to enforce strict military regulations. Why should he? Here in Lugdunum Convenarum, they were far from everything, and he was getting old and tired and he longed for the day he could retire and return to Rome, to his wife, and his children.

Valerius took his time: he heated the water, poured it, and took a few sips of the spicy brew. He wasn't toying with his men's impatience: he was giving himself time to think. He needed to decide what he should think of the events that had unfolded. What had happened that night had puzzled him, to say the least, and before he said anything he wanted to be sure that he had grasped all the facets of the situation. He knew instinctively that there were things he would not be able to understand, at least not yet; only the investigation could provide answers to the questions surrounding Cracius' death. The first question being, of course: "Who?"

"So, Valerius! What happened? They say Cracius was impaled on a dead branch when he fell off his horse?!"

"No, nobody's saying that anymore. It's the story Hadrianus had put out, at first. But Cracius was struck by a dagger, and, what's more, he was struck in the back. The Vespasiani's doctor saw it right away so Hadrianus had to admit that he had lied."

Canius, a decurion whose nickname was "Pot of Massilia" because he was born on the Phocean city and because his bones had been broken three times, twice during combat and a third time when he fell off a ladder when he was on guard duty, sat on his superior's camp bed and said:

"But why would he try to hide the fact that it was a crime?"

Valerius sighed. Flaccus, the short guy from Subura, in Rome, didn't give him time to answer.

"Did you find the weapon?"

"We did, and that's the problem: it was a Gallic dagger with a very long wooden handle, the kind they hold with both hands. They used them at the battle of Martico, you remember?"

"Gallic dogs. I knew there would be trouble."

Flaccus was among the Romans for whom a good Gaul was a dead Gaul. Maybe he'd seen too many wars to believe in peace anymore. To him, there would always be an occupier who had to rule by force and an occupied people who would rise up at every opportunity, at any sign of weakness. Valerius believed peace was possible; he tried to counter his men every time they made hasty judgments.

"Come, Flaccus, it's not a riot. A man was murdered; for now we don't know why, we don't know who. The weapon was a Gallic dagger, that's true, but we want to know whose hand wielded it. That's the important thing."

"What Roman would want to kill Cracius? He and his father have done so much for Lugdunum Convenarum."

'Flaccus is right, Valerius. The motive is the important thing; the Vespasiani have taken over so much arable land here that they have made enemies in half the farms of the region. If we're looking for motive, we should look among the expropriated peasants, and all of them are Gauls."

Valerius thought. They would be having this discussion over and over again. Who, why and how: these questions would keep him busy for the next few weeks. Valerius was only a soldier but he had power of police in the civitas. It wasn't his first investigation, but this one was very different in many ways. First and foremost was the character of the victim. Quintus had been very clear tonight: he was going to keep them both, Hadrianus and himself, under constant pressure. Usually, when a crime remained unexplained, a plebeian was picked at random to be exposed as an assassin and executed in front of a cheering crowd. This time, it wasn't going to be possible to commit such an error: Hadrianus was intent on preserving the peace, the Pax Romana. The Romans were in the midst of negotiations with the Convenes, hoping to secure their cooperation, and making headway, little by little. The Convenes knew this and would interpret the slightest injustice as a provocation and an affront. They would seize the opportunity to rekindle the rebellion.

Valerius ran his fingers through his hair a couple of times, and, then, finally, reacted to what Canius had said:

"How many Gallic warriors do you know who would strike someone in the back? You've fought them; they're savages; they have no sense of discipline, no notion of order. They fight dressed in rags; some don't even have a sword or a shield, just a dagger and a rock or even a stick, but they are brave. Only a traitor strikes from behind. Someone who does that is scared that his victim will recognize him and take his soul away."

"Why should a Roman be more of a coward than a Gaul? I don't know of any Roman soldier who would strike from behind."

"Not everyone is a soldier here, Canius. And then, what kind of Gaul leaves his dagger planted in his victim's back?"

Valerius looked up at the starry sky and listened to the dying sound of the crickets. It was late and tomorrow would be a long day. He blew out the candle he had set on the window sill because it was beginning to attract the night's insects. Canius and Flaccus both got up to return to their own quarters. They too were tired. Valerius had been determined to write his wife tonight, to send some news. He'd received a letter a month ago but hadn't yet found the time to respond. His wife was having trouble with their eldest son: he no longer wanted to be a soldier like his father. He'd got it into his head to find work in the new port. There was a time when Valerius would have hit the roof; he would have asked for a special leave to return to Rome and beat some sense into his son, remind him who was in charge – albeit from afar. But now Rome seemed so far away sometimes, as if shrouded in ever thickening mist as time passed. He'd never felt so tired of being a soldier , of never having a real place to live, of having to share everything with his men, rest, sleep and food, of having to sleep on make-shift beds and wearing clothes that didn't belong to him, of not owning anything, not even his own life... At the same time, he'd never felt so uncertain of ever being able to return home. The idea frightened him.

VII

Today, the sixteenth day before the calends of May: this afternoon, Cracius Vespasianus found dead on the blue peak, next to his horse, a dagger planted in his back. The body was discovered by the son of Harero, the Gallic shepherd from the hamlet by the bridge. No rigor mortis, no decomposition; the blood was coagulated but still dark red. According to the Vespasiani's doctor, Cracius was killed either that morning or during the night.

Fifteenth day before the calends of May: I've seen Harero; I've talked to all the people who live in the hamlet by the bridge; I questioned the Gauls who work the "Poplar" farm, on the slope facing the blue peak: nobody saw Cracius or anyone else. The Gauls are very reluctant to cooperate, not so much because they want to hide something but out of fear of being mixed up in the murder of a Roman aristocrat.

Fourteenth day before the calends of May: Hadrianus Trevius has ordered that Cracius' family not be questioned during the period of purification. In the meantime I'm going to concentrate on the young man's friends.

Eleventh day before the calends of May: I was able to meet Pompeius Melala, Balbius Iassus and Lucius Senica, all three members of Cracius' circle of friends. Only Sennius Basseus refused to see me on the pretext that he was sick. All three repeat the same story: they are completely astonished by what happened; they can't understand what could have happened. According to them Cracius had no enemies; he hadn't received any threats lately. I had the impression that their answers had been rehearsed and were being parroted out to me.

They described him as a free spirit, a good companion, and a generous friend. Even though it was true that Cracius wasn't directly involved in the business of the city or in his father's business and had no particular problem with the local population, he still had the reputation of being a debauched and scandalous young man, somewhat haughty and condescending, but, from what I gather, not more so than his four friends.

To conclude, the three young men willingly submitted to questioning but didn't show any real desire to help. I have the feeling that they're hiding something.

Ninth day before the calends of May: I was finally able to talk to Sennius Basseus whose statement was the same as the others'. My impression remains unchanged. I'll try and find out more about the doings of these young men.

Eighth day before the calends of May: the eight days of purification are over. Cracius' funeral will take place tomorrow.

VIII

The funeral cortege was more than a mile long; the flute players opened the march; the wailing women were beating their chests and pulling their hair. Their zeal was impressive: they almost tore their hair out. The Vespasiani must not have stinted on their fees.

There followed about twenty household slaves, who walked in silence. Three ladies in waiting held the funerary masks of Cracius' ancestors in front of their faces. Valerius was too far away to make out any detail but thought they had to be copies; the originals were most certainly in Rome, in Quintus' palace.

This was the biggest funeral ever held in Lugdunum Convenarum. People had come from all over to watch the event. Valerius would never have thought there were so many people living in the civitas. There were at least five thousand. He could make out, near the covered market, the Gallic peasants who had left their fields, the smiths who were clearly distinguished by their leather aprons and the potters: they had all arrived together. But who did they come to honor? What did they want to see? Most Gauls had never seen Cracius and were barely aware of the Vespasiani name. As for the Romans, their zeal was clearly due to curiosity, knowing, as they did, Cracius' reputation.

Or maybe there was something more. Valerius realized that it was the first time the entire city had gathered together. The first event that brought everyone out, peasants and city dwellers, slaves and citizens, plebeians and aristocrats, had to be a funeral. Would this ill fated day forever darken the future of Lugdunum Convenarum? The thought made him shudder. Cracius' body was laid out on a litter draped with black linen and carried by four bare-chested Numidians. Valerius knew that the Vespasiani had black slaves which they had brought from Africa, but he had never seen them until this day. They were really impressive: extremely tall and muscular, silent and impassive. The Gauls stepped back as they walked by; everyone looked at them as if they had just come out of the night. The presence of the priests walking on either side of the corpse re-assured the public; they were holding the effigies of the family gods of the Vespasiani in their hands. The family followed: Quintus of course and his wife Apronia on his arm and their daughter Lucilla. All three wore brown tunics. Quintus stood as straight as ever but his face, although perfectly still, betrayed him: he was an utterly broken man. Apronia was barely able to walk: Lucilla had both arms around her; the daughter was attempting to hold up the mother.

How can anyone ever get over that, Valerius wondered. Next came all the friends of the family: the Roman aristocracy first, then the richer tradesmen and craftsmen, and, finally, the Gallic dignitaries. Under orders from Hadrianus, Valerius had posted ten men who made up the rear of the procession in order to keep bystanders from joining the funeral. Some Roman citizens made a show of their displeasure at this measure which barred them from attending the funeral whereas some Gauls were among those allowed to march in it.

The wind that blows in from the Mediterranean sea and makes people go mad had stopped and now the wind that came from the ocean was going to bring rain. Grey clouds massed and then stretched over the mourners: they both advanced slowly eastward like two parallel processions, one hovering above the other and threatening it. *After all*, thought Valerius, *why not? Let it rain on these mourners, let it rain on the body and let Cracius' soul be cleansed and swept away in the flow*. He let his thoughts stray to the faint echo of his memory, so weak it wasn't sure what it should repeat before it died. He thought of his father whose funeral he could not attend, neither physically nor even from afar since he was told about his death three weeks after the cremation. His life as a soldier had kept him away from so many things! He'd been in Germania at the time. It was winter and the roads were impassable; even the army messengers couldn't get through. He remembered how much he had cried the day he had finally received the missive informing him of his father's death: he had felt like a child who has lost his parents in a crowd. Nothing could replace them; he felt abandoned and nothing could soothe him.

The flute players stopped playing: the column stood still and Valerius woke from his melancholy thoughts. The wailing women stood near the tomb that Quintus had had built on the road to Tolosa, at the head of an avenue lined with walnut trees. The name, Cracius Vespasianus Octavus, had been carved and blackened in the marble tombstone, under the inscription *Dis manibus* addressed to the dead. That way, the young man would be honored by the travelers passing his final resting place.

Valerius had moved up closer; he wanted to be nearer the procession. The litter was set down on the ground; Cracius' body had been wrapped in the black linen sheet he had been resting on and the precious bundle had been deposited in its receptacle, a granite sarcophagus whose fairly rough surface looked like it might tear the fine cloth. The empty litter looked flimsy and ridiculous next to the enormous mausoleum that Statitius Taurus, the stone cutter and his workers had hastily built for Quintus.

The small band of legionaries took up their positions, as planned, around the family. The priests intoned the prayers and Cracius' parents and their daughter took turns depositing their offerings for him, to persuade him to leave for the underworld until the time, during the Lemuria in May, when he could return. At that time there would be more offerings, more beautiful gifts so that Cracius' shade agreed to leave; then, his soul would rest in peace among the dead. Quintus gave the golden bracelet he'd been wearing for years, Apronia some balm of Judea in an alabaster bottle. Cracius always noticed its discreet yet heavy fragrance whenever she wore it. He could cause her terrible anxiety and disappoint her cruelly but she forgave him everything because of the way he looked at her, because he noticed even the slightest tremor in her heart, and even the perfume she wore. He'd glance at her and know how her heart felt; when he walked into her antechamber, it took him but a few seconds to notice that she was wearing a new scarf or that she had done her hair differently, to know whether she'd cried all night or whether this was going to be a good day. No other man, not even her husband had ever been as attentive to her. His powers of observation were part of his success with women. His mother knew he was heartless with them and knew no pity but that made her feel proud: she was his only love; she could boast of the everlasting love of a son. All these females got what they deserved when they mistook his insight for true feeling. They were the prey and he the hunter whereas, with her, he remained a child.

Never again could she wear that balm; much better that he take it with him in the other world: she didn't want any other living being to smell it on her.

Lucilla threw in a bouquet of blue cornflowers that she'd picked that morning, up there on the blue peak Cracius liked so much; she had tied them with the blue ribbon she was wearing the last time she saw her brother. It was the day before his death; she had asked where he was going: he didn't answer, just smiled and kissed her. She remembered how he had played with her hair and said: "Don't worry, little sister, that time will come soon enough for you too." Then, he had vanished around the corner of the domus.

Apronia thought the bouquet was in bad taste: that ill-fated peak that Cracius loved so much had been the cause of his death. But Lucilla had insisted and Quintus found the tribute moving, so Apronia had given in. In the end, what does it all matter, she pondered philosophically.

It had started to rain and Valerius cynically thought the inhumation would soon be over. Still, nobody among the official guests made a move. They were probably waiting for someone to be the first to leave, but no one dared. So they went on embracing each other, showing their pain, and praying to ward off the evil spirits.

Cracius' friends stood behind their parents. The whole group was there, standing in a circle: Pomponius Melala, Sennius Basseus, Lucius Senica and Balbius Iassus in the center. Cracius must have been the leader; he was the richest and his family had the most power and connections in Rome but more than that: his qualities, his beauty, his charisma and his talent for partying, the imagination he displayed in order to break out of the monotony of provincial life, all that made him the natural leader of the small band of cynical young aristocrats.

Balbius Iassus looked as if he might be the next leader of the group. He stood in the center, he spoke and the others listened. He appeared to be giving them instructions, as if he were trying to convince them of something, or maybe even to reassure them. Valerius was too far removed to hear what they were saying; he could only try and read their faces but he thought he could learn more by watching them from afar. He could have been mistaken but he felt that he could detect, along with their very legitimate show of sadness at having lost a friend, an atmosphere of nervous conspiracy. He couldn't help but think, as he had when he questioned them that those four knew much more than they cared to tell him. Maybe he was wrong; maybe what he saw were real, physical expressions of sorrow; that was possible as well. But to him, they just looked like four little cubs in the wilderness who had suddenly been alerted to danger by a crackling twig in a thicket, far away, or by an unknown scent carried over by the wind.

Hadrianus and Claudia were present of course. More than the death of a loved one, they were mourning the good match they thought they had secured for their daughter. Valerius had the impression that Cracius hadn't been very high in Hadrianus' esteem, apart from his fortune and his illustrious family. Together with the Iassi, the Melalae, the Bassei and the Senicae, the Magistrate and his wife stood round Quintus and Apronia. While their sons could appear to be frightened little chicks, their parents were accomplished predators, the Empire's birds of prey. They were the pillar of Roman aristocracy in the city, the six richest families in this region of Aquitania, and all power was concentrated in their hands.

The young men's sisters had joined Lucilla. Staia seemed to hold a special place in her heart: the two young women would have become sisters in law and a deep bond held them together today. Friendship was transmitted from generation to generation in aristocratic circles. The families were united by bonds of affection as well as common interests; marriage and wealth went hand in hand.

Hadrianus had left his wife and friends to walk over to Valerius and talk to him. He surprised the centurion in his thoughts.

"What are you looking at so intently that you didn't even hear me coming, Valerius?"

"Nothing in particular. I was thinking."

"How sad, isn't it? What a tragic end. He died so young."

How sad for you and your daughter, thought Valerius. *You won't find any better match for her.*

Hadrianus drew his hand over his face and pulled on the slightly sagging skin under his jowls. This was no vain attempt to smooth out the years; he didn't care about his physique and had never exercised as some men liked to do. Claudia had reproached him from time to time and pointed to some of their friends who did: Eutrapelus and Gallicus exercised every day before their ablutions and Quintus Vespasianus still practiced boxing. What preoccupied him at that moment was not his weight, it was the investigation: he would have preferred to avoid it but now he was duty bound to supervise it. He didn't want a Gaul to be implicated: that would destroy the peaceful relations he'd worked so long to establish. But he also didn't want Valerius to bother the Roman aristocracy of Lugdunum Convenarum. Valerius had questioned Cracius' friends before the funeral; now he was standing very close to the Vespasiani and kept observing the young men so pensively: Hadrianus didn't like that at all. He knew Valerius had always been a faithful servant of the Quattuorvirate but he also knew that he was capable of carrying his sense of duty too far and of making no concessions in the pursuit of his mission; he was very much a military man. That was the reason why Hadrianus was rubbing his face: he was searching for words to tell Valerius, without antagonizing him, that he didn't want him probing too closely.

"I was told you questioned Balbius Iassus, Pomponius Melala and Lucius Senica a few days ago."

"Yes. Sennius Basseus, also. They're...they were friends of Cracius. I wanted to know whether Cracius had enemies, whether he'd been threatened lately. Since you stopped me from seeing the Vespasiani until after the funeral, I thought the young men would be able to give the best information. I didn't want to waste any time."

"You know, Valerius, there's no urgency. I prefer that you take your time with this investigation; don't rush things."

"Time is running against me, on the contrary. I only have seventeen days left, as you know."

"I can persuade Quintus to be patient. If your investigation quickly turns up some elements, if you find a lead, I can bring him back to his senses and he'll go back on his ultimatum."

"For now I haven't found anything. But I have the impression that these four are hiding something from me." Valerius indicated Cracius' friends with a discreet tilting of his chin but it wasn't discreet enough for Hadrianus who didn't want anyone guessing about the subject of their conversation; the centurion was a little too visible for his taste and, placing an arm on his shoulder, he led him away from Cracius' family and friends.

"They're young and they're still in shock. That's understandable: they've never had to deal with the death of a close friend."

"Yes, but now, I hope Cracius' parents and his sister will be more forthcoming and that I'll learn more from them."

"I'm not sure it's a good idea to go after the Vespasiani now. I talked to Quintus; he has no idea who could have committed this horrible crime. Apronia doesn't either. I think it best, in any case, that you avoid harassing them with your questions."

"How can I conduct a real investigation if I can't question the victim's relatives?"

"Take the investigation in a different direction; start gathering the statements of witnesses who are outside the circle of the Vespasiani."

"But I can't very well question witnesses who haven't seen anything or didn't even know Cracius."

"Everybody knew Cracius, which is what makes your mission difficult... There are many possible witnesses outside the Vespasiani family."

"You can't be serious, Hadrianus."

"I'm absolutely serious, Valerius."

The meaning of those words frightened the centurion. He looked the First Magistrate straight in the eye and he forced himself, with his big soldier's body, covered in leather and metal, to keep completely still so as not to betray any surprise or disapproval, then, calmly, deliberately, he said: "I mustn't look for the culprit among the rich Roman families, correct?"

Hadrianus wasn't the kind of man who would let an inferior stare him down; he wasn't much bothered by scruples; he didn't see the point of volunteering unnecessary explanations. He didn't owe any to Valerius but he disliked the man's question precisely because it wasn't out of bounds, it didn't even challenge the respect due to his rank. "And you mustn't look among the rich Gallic families either."

He didn't need to add "That's an order." His tone made it sufficiently clear. It was the second time in a couple of days that he had used his authority to intimidate the centurion. This had never happened before and Valerius reflected that there really were quite a few troubling aspects in the matter of Cracius' death; it was as if all the aristocrats of Lugdunum Convenarum stood to gain by keeping things quiet. With feigned naiveté, very close to insubordination, he demanded:

"Tell me how I can track down the murderer if I can't interrogate anyone, I can't indict anyone and I can't put anyone behind bars."

"You may do all that as much as you please, Valerius, but not among any of the great Gallic or Roman families of the city."

The Vespasiani's servants had gone home to finish preparing for the funeral banquet in honor of the dead man. Only the relatives remained. The clouds had finally burst and big drops of cold rain swept by the wind penetrated through the fine cloth of the togas and the tunics.

Valerius respected Hadrianus as a man, but he detested politicians. He understood all that was left unsaid behind the magistrate's words; it was a language he knew but one that he refused to speak. His own words spoke of honor versus disgrace, victory or defeat, reward or punishment. He found it hard not to throw the words he really wanted to use in Hadrianus' face, but, in the end, he let it go. He made one last attempt, without much conviction and when he spoke, it was in the voice of a disappointed child:

"I don't understand what harm just asking a few questions..."

"Since when is a centurion expected to understand? Your duty is to obey."

Hadrianus realized he'd spoken out loud and immediately turned around to check if anyone had overheard. The years he had spent in the inner circle of power and in the magistracy had taught him how to command respect. But, during those years, he had also learned that it was always better to persuade than to compel. And so, in order to ensure that Valerius would be on his side, he pretended to take him into his confidence; he drew closer and said, as if speaking to a friend he could trust:

"I can't afford to rekindle a war with the Convenes. I need a perfect culprit; choose anyone, but quickly. Find some miserable bastard every one can hate, some beggar passing through, or a slave or an ex-convict... whoever, but not a citizen, and not a Gallic nobleman."

"But Hadrianus, why don't you give me a little time first to establish the facts, to gather clues, to find out whether Cracius had a quarrel with anyone or if he had creditors, or if someone owed him money. Let me dig around. I'm sure I can come up with something; I know I can find the murderer. His friends are hiding something, I'm convinced of it."

"His friends won't tell you anything, Valerius. They don't feel like talking to you; they want to be left alone and you shall not bother them."

Hadrianus couldn't care less who the real killer was; all he wanted was for the city to continue living peacefully and for Lugdunum Convenarum to preserve its good name.

"Don't you realize how disastrous it would be for our little city if the Proconsul were to find out that a member of the Vespasiani family has been murdered by a Roman citizen or a Gallic nobleman? No, that can't happen; it has to be a heinous crime committed by some lowlife whom we will promptly unmask and put to death on the rack for all to see. Some people in Burdigala are waiting for the smallest misstep on our part so that they can seize the district, put it under their supervision and rob us of its management."

"Quintus is not going to be satisfied with a substitute culprit; he'll want to make him confess, and he'll see through the deception very quickly."

"He won't have time to talk to him: the murderer will attempt to escape during the arrest and he'll be killed as he was struggling to get away."

"What?"

This time, Valerius was the one to raise his voice, but he didn't care whether he was heard or not. Hadrianus glanced at the group of friends. Apronia and Lucilla were instructing two slaves who had almost finished arranging the flowers around the grave and placing the offerings from the family's friends and from the Gallic delegation inside the tombstone. The priests were still there, standing in the pouring rain, waiting for the trapdoor to the tomb to be sealed. Slaves came running back from town bringing large sheets to hold over their masters' heads and protect them from the rain on their return to the upper city. Everyone hurried and no one paid any attention to Hadrianus and Valerius, apart, maybe, from Claudia, Hadrianus' wife, who gestured to her husband that she wished to return home.

"I refuse to order my men to kill an innocent man in cold blood."

"You won't have to: you'll be the one to do it."

Hadrianus jabbed at the centurion's leather armor with his index finger; Valerius had involuntarily stepped forward, his chest swollen, in defiance of the Magistrate.

Claudia had come up to them to ask again that they leave because she was cold but she noticed that the two men were not having a friendly exchange: she stopped. She heard Hadrianus say to Valerius:

"It's an order, centurion. And you better carry it out without a word to anyone else unless you prefer to end your career somewhere in deepest Africa, as a simple legionary."

Valerius gave up. Hadrianus, although he was half his size, kept jabbing at him with his finger so he backed away. He knew only too well that if he said any more it would become insubordination and that could be considered an act of treachery. Those were not empty threats. Valerius knew of officers who had ended up in the galleys for less; even a general would hesitate to speak to Hadrianus the way Valerius, who was only a centurion, just had.

He avoided the First Magistrate's eyes. He watched the stone cutters closing Cracius' tomb: the sarcophagus vanished behind the granite wall. Was the secret of the young man's death being sealed for all eternity? When Valerius turned to go,

Hadrianus had already walked away. He disappeared behind a wall of rain, hurrying to catch up with Claudia.

Only Valerius and his men, who had taken shelter under their shields, stood by the tomb now. He himself was drenched to the bone. The Vespasiani and their friends were going to carouse into the night. They were going to eat and drink to forget their sorrows and accompany Cracius on his final journey, and do those things that Cracius had loved so much.

But what could the centurion do? With whom could he share his feelings of disgust?

He thought of Serenia, of the children, of their house not far from the Tiber, at the foot of the Janiculum hill. It wasn't a real domus, but neither was it a simple insula. It was a small house and it belonged to them; it had no garden and no inside courtyard; it was a little dark and humid, but there were flowers and the walls were covered with ivy.

At that moment, as he stood in the pouring rain, he had only one wish: to go back to the fort, to dry himself, to drink a large bowl of beer and then go to bed.

IX

In the days that followed everyone tried to go back to their normal routine. Hadrianus convened the council again to complete the debates on the financing of the network for drinking water and the sewer system. The tragic events that had interrupted the first meeting had also put a stop to the rancor between the Romans, the Convenes, the tradesmen and the aristocrats. The council had become a united and silent body where the only things that were discussed were concurring points of view and essential information. The mood in the curia was solemn.

Hadrianus, pragmatic as ever, took the opportunity to introduce his plan for a trophy in honor of Augustus. Not only was there no opposition, but he was even granted a substantial sum. He was going to commission a group of statues; the white marble from Passus Lupus would be carved in Ollion's famous workshop in Rome, after a drawing by Plautus Silvanus.

Verus, the local sculptor complained that he hadn't been given the commission but Hadrianus retorted bluntly: "We want to flatter Augustus, not you." The answer was followed by silence and the First Magistrate's decision was unanimously approved.

After a few rainy days, sunshine returned but far fewer people went to the forum than before Cracius' death. The atmosphere had changed: there was no taste for strolling; a persistent disquiet had spread over the city, from the muddy alleys of the lower town to the shady lanes separating the walled gardens of the rich up above on the heights.

Valerius wasn't resigned: he couldn't give up the search for the murderer, he couldn't allow an innocent man to die in his place. He did what he could to find some explanation, some clues towards identifying the culprit, all without overstepping the limits that Hadrianus had set him. He'd returned to the top of the peak to study traces and footprints in the grass in an attempt to piece together what had really happened up there; but the footprints of all the people who had gone there after Cracius' death had mixed and the rain made it so much worse. It was now impossible to differentiate those that might have been left by the murderer. He'd also gone back to the Gallic hamlet but the young shepherd told him nothing new. The centurion's recurring visits had quickly displeased the peasants: they were in any case reluctant to speak to Romans and they were worried about what people might think of them if the centurion was seen coming in the village too often. As a matter of fact, everyone avoided Valerius. It was well known that he was looking for the murderer and so they all did their best to avoid speaking to him.

At the fort, his men found him more taciturn than ever. The terrible secret that he had to keep weighed on him and he found it difficult to conceal his disgust. He felt a nauseating sickness inside: he saw himself as the arm of a rotting body; and that body's head was ordering the other arm to cut off the first one if it failed or disobeyed. He was the product of a system that would make him commit an impious act. The nausea sometimes gave way to a feeling of revolt. But, after his anger and disgust had passed, he was left only with an immense lassitude.

He felt all the more helpless as he could no longer see where he should begin his investigation. He would have liked to question Staia, Hadrianus' daughter, but it was impossible to even mention her name in front of him. He had to pretend she'd never been engaged to Cracius; he had to deny the possibility that the young man could have confided in her or even that she might have seen him on that fateful day.

Cracius' sister Lucilla could also have been her brother's confidant. Maybe she had been even closer to him than Staia herself. But, once again, Valerius was persona non grata at the house of the Vespasiani and he couldn't ask any questions there.

As for Cracius' friends, they had probably been told that it would be best to stay at home and if Valerius had thought he could pretend to run into them by chance, that too was now impossible. In order to talk to them he would have to flout Hadrianus' orders; but even then, he could never get past the door of the Iassi, the Melalae, the Bassei, the Senicae and any such families. For the moment, he stood in the sun, by the oppidum's palisade, on the parapet walk. The sagging wooden planks groaned under his weight. Noises came up from the camp: the legionaries were washing, sweeping the floors or cooking. He liked coming out here: it was like standing on a border between the inside and the outside, between a well ordered world safely hidden from prying eyes, and the chaotic and perilous world beyond. He felt at home, here, in his fort; he could observe what was happening below in the Roman city, down in the lower city and further away in the valley. He could see storms forming on the summits of the Pyrenees before they blew over the city; he liked to watch the peasants working in the fields; he even thought he could make out the shimmering waters of the Garonne, far away in the distance.

Wheat had started growing and would soon ripple in the wind. He heard the stone cutters working on the baths, adjusting the boulders that were going up day by day. A few lonely columns stood in the middle of what seemed to be the main body of a building, probably a gymnasium. The three different baths were already clearly visible but it was still hard to imagine how the scaffolding would turn into a vast thermal complex capable of serving the ever increasing population of Lugdunum Convenarum. Beyond that, Valerius could barely make out the stalls around the forum. He spotted the chimney over Cracus' bakery; it was out for now. What he could see clearly were the barrels the Gauls piled up to twenty feet high: the heights had increased perilously after Augustus imposed a tax on the ground surface of all the shops in the provinces. One of the piles erected by the barrel makers of Lugdunum Convenarum had collapsed after a sudden storm and seriously wounded a child, prompting Hadrianus to regulate their height.

Valerius knitted his dark brows. He resembled a statue, a tall, motionless silhouette, with a massive, powerful chest, towering over the palisade. Like a statue, he could be broken but would not bend.

From where he was standing, he could have almost recognized Lorus and Hadrianus walking together in the forum. One of them was holding three sheets with drawings of vertical ornaments and human figures with dimensions and notes in the margins; the other carried what looked like a blue-print of the city. It was too far for Valerius to make out their faces, but he could have recognized those two familiar silhouettes: Hadrianus' rotund, opulent shape, his way of arching his back and advancing with an air of extreme hauteur; Lorus Divolus' thin stooping frame, his halting steps, pro-gressing nervously, then swerving off suddenly to the side, as if he were forever attempting to vanish. Both were instantly recognizable.

The two men were different in every way; when their hands touched in the act of holding down the documents against the wind, the Magistrate's plump hands made the manager's dry fingers look like claws. Their hands were a reflection of their lives: an easy, soft life for Hadrianus and a harried, tough existence for the former slave. Hands that gave orders and hands that served. The people they came across, a few farmers returning from the ninth hour market, carrying bags of the first chard of the season, slaves and Gauls going back to their work, were surprised to see them at that time of day. The First Magistrate had made it a rule not to go out before the afternoon, after his nap and after his bath. If they were walking about so early in the afternoon, it had to be for an important reason. So people saluted them and tried to steal a glance at the mysterious drawings. What could those two be up to? All around, the only thing one could see were the brick layers working on the site of the future baths: probably Hadrianus had wanted to check personally how much progress was being made. No one could have guessed that there was a much different reason for the two men's presence. They were not simply trying to picture the beautiful thermal establishment that would soon rise in this empty space; they were trying to imagine the great circle that would be laid out south of the city, at the intersection of the road to Tolosa and the road to Iberia through the Pyrenees. There, at the crossroads, would stand the huge sculpture Plautius Silvanus had drafted on the very documents they were holding. Picturing something out of nothing was hard for Lorus: he believed only in numbers, in things he could see. But it was easy for Hadrianus whose megalomania easily fueled his imagination.

He could just picture the monument to Augustus, standing right there, below the citadel, at the entrance to the city. It would be the largest trophy ever erected! Not just one tower, but three symmetrical monuments each commemorating

Augustus' great victories: one for his victory over Antony and
Cleopatra at Actium, another to celebrate the defeat of the
Cantabri and the Astures and a third one representing
vanquished Gaul. Thus would Augustus' destiny preside over
the city's future. Rome's peace, Pax Romana, would be carved
in stone in Lugdunum Convenarum and the city would become
the keystone of the three provinces of Narbonensis, Aquitania
and Tarraconensis.

From his vantage point, high up on the oppidum, Valerius
couldn't make out any of this. His thoughts were elsewhere. He
surveyed the vast expanse of fields, the forests beyond and the
immense rock barrier that closed the horizon from the east to
the west. There was too much nature here, and he found it
oppressive. He let melancholy engulf him. He missed children's
cries, he missed the stinking, overcrowded alleys of Rome; he
wished he could go fishing with his brother on the banks of the
Tiber, the way they used to when they were young boys. At this
time of year, the Tiber would be replenished; sometimes it
even overflowed. He remembered eating fresh fish in Ostia,
playing tali with the neighborhood children on the ledge of the
temple fountain and watching the little knuckle bones bounce
gaily off the mossy green stone and fall in the water with a soft
plop that made you feel like jumping in with your clothes on.
You'd have to stick your arm as deep as possible into the water
to catch them. Every one tried to grab them before they
reached the bottom and it always ended in a big messy
splashing fight while the game of tali was forgotten.

Valerius would have given anything to go back, just for a
moment, to the Esquiline and finish the game of knuckle
bones with the children; he stood still, stealing one more
minute of past joy from the present.

He started walking along the palisade, out of habit, as he
had walked all these years as a legionary. The sentry's tired step,
counting time with his feet, yearning to be relieved, came back

to him naturally: right foot falling in exactly the same spot as during the previous round, left foot stepping on the same knot in the wooden plank, on the same pattern in the wood. The faces of his fellow soldiers from the days when he was a legionary stationed in Germania came back to him: Julius Apollinarius, who had died in Argentorate, his skull split in two by a German's axe, right under Valerius' eyes - he himself had barely escaped a second blow from the barbarian and had made it to safety by running into the forest; Tacitus Publius, whose body was never found when he disappeared in the frozen waters of a lake in Rhetia; Campanus and Alleuis, who, like Valerius, had made it. He thought of all the others whose names had disappeared, the ones he'd forgotten about and, strangely, remembering them hurt him more: it was like a stab in the heart. They were an army of ghosts scattered across the empire so that Rome could build roads and bleed the provinces and enrich the aristocracy of the Latium. Valerius never forgot that the first blood that had been shed was that of the tens of thousands of Roman legionaries.

He would have liked to go on reminiscing but a feeling of anxiety was gnawing at him. He couldn't define it at first. As he went down the ladder he thought about everything that could have caused it; it quickly came back to him, clear as day: the investigation, the impossibility of questioning the people who were implicated, the fact that the culprit would remain unpunished and that he himself would have to designate a victim, an innocent man, and kill him. For a short time, he had managed to forget all about that.

With an air of determination, he strode across the courtyard when in fact he had nowhere to go. He took the opportunity to scold the team on cleaning duty: it was unwarranted but he needed to do something, out of exasperation.

Cracius' death, Hadrianus' orders, the Vespasiani, the shortened investigation he was ordered to conduct to make a show of searching for the culprit, all that enraged him.

He'd sent his decurions on three patrols on a token search of the farms to find some hypothetical vagabond; they questioned the farmers who might have seen a foreigner or a suspect lurking around recently. Another patrol made the rounds of the merchants and the artisans in the city. Valerius knew perfectly well that this was pointless but he had to show that he was doing something and that the trail he was following was that of a criminal outsider who had intended to rob Cracius of his money.

His men might come across some poor drunken bugger with a few stolen silver coins who happened to be passing through and they would find that the coins belonged to Cracius. Everything would fit: the man's profile, the motive and the evidence; with a little persuasion, the man would confess and then he would be quartered in the forum. If he refused to admit to the crime, Valerius would have to follow the plan thought up by Hadrianus and kill him on the pretext that he had attempted to escape during questioning.

In the event, this seemed the better solution to Valerius because he wouldn't be compelled to pick an innocent man from the local community, whose members he had known for years.

He reached the officers' quarters. It was quiet inside. That was so seldom the case that Valerius stood still for a few moments to listen to the silence, as if he were seeing the place in a new light. He pushed aside the curtain to his room, looked at his bed and wondered whether he would take a nap, but he decided he was too upset to sleep, so he opened his chest, took out his belt and his helmet, adjusted his sword against his hip and left the building. He should have taken advantage of this moment of peace and quiet to write his wife Serenia, but solitude wasn't enough; he also needed peace of mind and that, he didn't have.

He walked over to the stables; there were only a few horses for the mail. He asked the Gaul, an expert in curing horses with plants who also served as a cook in the camp, to saddle his horse. A foot soldier didn't usually ride, not even a centurion. Riding was, of course, a privilege of the members of the knightly class but Hadrianus had suspended the rule and allowed him to use a horse because of the vast distances he had to cover throughout the district. Valerius had been compelled to learn to ride and the camp had had a good laugh at his expense for several weeks. The legionary's large frame, built for long marches and for fighting seemed huge on the horse. Valerius' military stiffness was completely unsuited to the horse's graceful gait but the animal must have been particularly docile: he didn't throw off the soldier, who seemed to stay in the saddle by some miracle. Riding was as natural to Valerius as flying would have been for a camel. And yet, little by little, he and the horse had gotten accustomed to each other and ended up as excellent friends; in moments of disillusionment or doubt, such as now, the stallion was his only source of comfort. He'd come to prefer his company to that of his decurions.

The strange pair rode around the courtyard for no reason and then left. The groom looked at the rider's back: it was bent too far forward; he looked at his knees: they weren't tight enough. The centurion, perched on his horse, was a hopelessly funny sight.

Valerius never galloped; he trotted down the hill from the fortress toward the blue peak. He rode through a pasture where a few grazing sheep immediately scattered, forded a shimmering brook, entered a beech wood and then reached a hill planted with oaks. The blue peak stood a little higher still; it was bare save for the magnificent great oak at the center, on the highest point of the peak, its trunk dark and forbidding.

The oaks were just starting to fill out but the musty odors of the undergrowth, freed from the grip of winter, filled the air and the mushrooms were ready to grow at the first burst of sunshine. Here, under the trees, the dampness of spring was stronger and the sound of the horse's hooves was muffled.

Valerius was hoping to find some peace up here or maybe some inspiration. Who could tell? Maybe Cracius' soul was still hiding in the grass or hovering in the wind: would it whisper the name of his murderer?

Once he had reached the very top of the peak, he climbed awkwardly off his horse and tied him to the tree. The grass had grown very high because the Gauls no longer dared to take their sheep to this pasture. The place was cursed and they feared being questioned again if they were seen there.

Standing with his hands on his hips, Valerius admired the Pyrenees. The snowy peaks sparkled in the sun and almost blinded him. Maybe Cracius was standing here just like this when he was stabbed. Instinctively, Valerius swung around and then immediately thought: 'Shame on you!'

He lay down in the grass: under him, the damp earth, above him, the tree, and through the branches, the sky.

That had probably been the last thing Cracius had seen before he'd closed his eyes forever. But he must also have seen something else: the face of his murderer, bending over him, watching him slowly die.

If only the oak tree could speak!

The grass tickled his face. The setting sun reddened their yellow tips. Valerius sat up, turned toward the city and wondered how long it would be before the shadow of the hills darkened its streets. He pulled up a blade of grass, stuck it between his teeth and resolved to stay until that time. Later, much later, he would ride back down.

X

Dear Serenia:
        A blue bird just flew past the window, and yet, it's late; night has fallen.

Could it be a sign you are sending me, a message from beyond the mountains, from the opposite shore of the sea? Or is it a creature of the day that my nocturnal brooding has disturbed? I can't really think anymore. Maybe the absence of thought can keep you awake just as too much disquiet does. Maybe that's what people mean when they speak of "dark thoughts": a feeling of emptiness in your head, when there are no thoughts to knock around inside your skull, when there's nothing left inside but the darkness of your soul.

Will these words frighten you or seem ridiculous, or will you think me mad, after an absence of two years, two years without seeing you?

I don't know how to write to you anymore. I can't write. Writing seems incongruous or dishonest, as if I were an impostor passing himself off as your husband and writing you under an assumed name. Will you recognize Musa, the centurion, when you get this letter or should I spare you and destroy it like all the others, all the others you never received and that make you think I've forgotten you?

I'm so afraid, Serenia. How can I come back to you? What can I say to you?

Do I exist outside this fort? It's been the measure of my life for so long. It feeds me; it tells me what to do and how to do it; it tells me when to speak and when to be silent.

And our boys, who are they? What am I now to them? Am I still a small part of your family? Have I ever been?

The glory of Rome has called me far away from you; it has demanded that I sacrifice everything to it. All these years, I've believed in the glory of Rome, I abandoned my family for the sake of that glory. And now I wonder: has all this been for the good of just a few people, has this glorious ideal been nothing but a great hoax?

It's all very confusing. I'm tired of this life but I don't know any other.

XI

"Do you love me?"

The young man didn't answer. He was looking at his limp penis resting on its side. He was proud of his appendage: it performed very well. But it was going to have to do more and live up to its reputation.

"You do love me, don't you?"

With a sigh and barely disguising his boredom, he answered: "Yes, of course I do."

He gazed at his abdominal muscles that rippled under the skin and kept his stomach flat. He fondled his bulging chest muscles, his well oiled torso and his manly but not over abundant body hair. The girl watched him; she would have preferred that he caress her. She came closer, pressed her body against his, nestling into every hollow she could fill.

This girl was exasperating; she was so demanding and intrusive. He pretended to stretch so he could push her away, without appearing to do so; then, saying he needed to drink, he got up, leaving her on the rumpled bed.

She didn't dare make any more demands. And yet she yearned to talk to him, to question him. She would have liked to know whether his indifference was normal, whether all men were like that. Was it normal for her not to want to be pushed away and discarded after having been so passionately desired? Should she stop hoping for anything better and should she just keep quiet?

She felt so unsure of what to expect and yet so close to the real question: did Balbius really love her? Was this love? He offered her a cup of wine from Alba Helvia that he had brought up from the family cellar where his father kept it in barrels.

"One more benefit of Roman civilization, my dear," he said and offered her the cup. The young woman, not used to drinking wine, refused. He had already made her drink earlier in the evening and it had turned her stomach and almost made her lose her senses.

Balbius' voice was already slurred by drink. She wished he wouldn't drink so much. Earlier that evening, she had noticed how, after a few drinks, he had looked at her differently. She hoped it wasn't just drink that made him desire her, but, apparently, this too was part of the ritual of seduction, of love. Should she have refused him? But, even if she had wanted to, would she have been able to? He would certainly have accused her of being one those kill-joy Gallic girls he and his friends sometimes made fun of. Roman girls, by comparison, seemed so liberated, so free! To them, the Gauls' modesty was so ridiculous and uncivilized. She'd even heard that Roman women liked to display objects of intimate pleasure and that they talked freely about their lovemaking. Her friends who worked for Roman families had told her all this.

Balbius had been so kind, so careful. She had never done it before and, even though she was clumsy, he had reassured her, helped her, and told her how he felt honored that she had given herself to him; he said that he liked the fact that she hadn't known any other man before him; who cared if she lacked expertise, feelings were what counted. The man she'd discovered tonight had been so gentle, so different from what people were saying about the young Roman aristocrats of the city.

And then, there were so many young women hanging around him, just as beautiful as she was and much richer and they came from families of his own class. How lucky she was, how honored she felt that he should have chosen her among all the others. For a young woman of the lower Gallic nobility, to be loved by someone like Balbius Iassus was well worth some sacrifice! It meant a great alliance and a dazzling, unexpected social promotion. She would become a citizen; she would be married in a marble palace; she would leave her parents' 'Romanesque' house and live in a real 'domus' full of slaves and sculptures. She would have a hairdresser to take care of her long tawny mane that the Romans were so enthralled with and she would make her hair shine so that her friends would be livid with envy! And she would have a dresser and a seamstress to make her the most beautiful dresses with cotton from Titus' shop or even fine wool that she would order from Mateus' in Tolosa. She would travel throughout the Empire and visit Rome, at Balbius' side, carried in a sedan chair.

Her feelings of melancholy, her need for tenderness and for words of affection after the love making seemed to pale compared to such magnificent prospects. She would find ways to make him desire her loving attention; she would soften his heart. Women knew how to work their charms on men; they didn't need expensive potions or magic balms.

Ah, but Balbius had returned to her again. He'd put his wine cup down at the foot of the bed, on the glazed earth flagstones. Again, he was looking at her with love in his eyes; his gaze was gentle, just as it had been when they'd made love the first time, a short time before.

He brushed his forehead against her lower leg and kissed her very softly on the foot. She shuddered slightly, it tickled but it felt wonderful and she didn't want him to stop. His lips were opening and his kisses became stronger; she felt his mouth open on her skin. Now, he was licking the arch of her left foot, then her right foot. His tongue darted between her toes as she tried hard not to giggle for fear he would think her silly. All her toes were now in his mouth, as if he wanted to swallow her foot whole. His breathing had become harder. He bit her ankles and with his tongue lapping at her shins, reached behind her knee, and, stealthily, up inside her thigh.

"Mm, it's warm here, it's soft. You're so soft all over," he whispered.

She felt a wave of pleasure rise inside her. She couldn't have said what she liked the most: his warm, moist mouth on the inside of her thighs, the nearness of her vulva aching for him, or the words he had just uttered. She had spread her legs apart slightly for him, but not enough, he thought. Softly still, but firmly, he said: "Open up, more."

She let him guide her.

Earlier in the evening their love making had been very soft; he had been on top of her. She had slipped beneath the sheets after taking her clothes off and he had joined her, lying down next to her, and he had started stroking her hair, then caressing her shoulders, as if he were exploring her skin with his hands as much as with his eyes. He told her that her skin was so white it was almost transparent: 'diaphanous', he said. She didn't know that word but it must have been a compliment. He had caressed her breasts, then between her legs and he had slipped on top of her so that she had felt his penis, now hard and so big. She had wondered whether all men had a big penis like that when they had an erection. He had taken his time, he had been delicate, and little by little, he had penetrated her, moving up and down and she was so happy that he seemed to enjoy being inside her so much. All of a sudden, he had stopped, had groaned and she had felt his semen emptying into her. Everything had happened the way she had been told. It had hurt a little but not much. She barely had time to enjoy the weight of his body on her, the warmth of his breath on her neck. He had fallen over on his back and hadn't talked to her and had stopped caressing her. His eyes became distant and cold. She thought she must have done something wrong.

This time it wasn't the same. He was in love with her again. His breathing grew harder. He crushed her breasts with more abandon but without ever hurting her. He had grabbed her hand and forced her to hold his penis; he wanted her to hold it tight.

"Tighter; don't be afraid, hold it tighter. Ah, yes, that's it, just like that." She didn't say a word. She complied.

With a thrust of his head, a bit like a ram, he pushed her thighs wide open. He put his hands under her and lifted her up and held her with her legs up in the air and her crotch wide open. Suddenly, she felt completely naked, and she held her breath. She would have preferred to close her legs, to hide herself. She closed her eyes, not wanting to see his eyes gazing at her there. And yes, Balbius' eyes were wide open; he was looking at her and seemed filled with wonder. He reveled at the sight of her, like a man about to devour some delectable dish, or like a child who'd just been given a beautiful present. Holding her up, he bent over her and deposited a few fluttering kisses all around her Venus mound and her flesh tingled with delight. Circling closer and closer, he reached her labia and started licking her more and more precisely. Her whole body quivered. She had never felt such intense pleasure. Never when she touched herself, had she experienced such tremors. Unable to suppress the sounds she heard coming from her, moaning sounds like the mysterious ones she had heard filtering from her parents' room.

Balbius was seized then by a sort of madness. He too seemed in the grip of some uncontrollable frenzy: this scared her a little but she didn't dislike it. Now he was rubbing his face against her groin, kissing her, feasting on her, taking in her scent, and what seeped from her. He slipped his fingers inside, in her anus and in her vulva at the same time and went on licking her: she couldn't tell anymore where her pleasure came from. She loved it when his tongue paused for a moment where she was taught and swollen like a grape on the point of bursting. It was so strong that it almost hurt.

Balbius seemed truly enchanted by her body and she thought she was probably not doing so badly after all. She gained some confidence and she sensed that maybe now it was her turn to take the initiative. So she did what she'd been told would satisfy a man: she did what he was doing to her, and, in the heat of their passion, in the brutality of their embrace, in all the noise they were both making, she forgot herself, she forgot her reluctance and her disgust. She even started liking it, liking his vital, warm strength in her mouth. She felt an immense joy that she had become a woman; what she held between her lips was the most intimate and the most fragile part of Balbius. He had granted her that privilege; he trusted her, he loved her.

They made love late into the night promising each other everlasting love: every night would be sweet and warm like tonight, the strength of their love would knock down every barrier, it would overcome all the obstacles they encountered before they could marry openly.

"Above all, promise me you won't tell anyone, not even Cevila. If ever it came out that we are together, it would be a disaster."

"I swear, Balbius, no one will know. But our parents are going to have to know someday since we want to get married."

"Yes, but my family isn't ready for that yet. It isn't accepted that a Iassus marry outside the Roman aristocracy. They might repudiate me, disinherit me. Let me build up my own fortune first and then we'll be free from my parents."

"Oh, Balbius, my love, how long do you think we'll have to live like this? How long will we have to hide?"

"I don't know, Lemei. But the important thing is that we love each other. We'll have the rest of our lives to be together officially. So for now we can afford to be a little patient, don't you agree?"

She snuggled up closer. He was so strong, so handsome. Of course she would wait, of course she would be patient.

"But what if I get pregnant?"

"What are you talking about? We'll be careful."

"Yes, but even so. It can happen."

"We'll see. There are sorceresses who know how to flush them out with potions."

"Balbius, Balbius, I love you so much. I can't wait to give you a son. I'll make you the happiest man in the Roman empire."

The young man looked at her with a condescending little smile. He put her hand on his cheek, and then laid it against his chest. He had had his fill. Now, all he wanted was to sleep but there was one more thing he had to do before the sun rose and before he sent her back home. He ran his fingers through her hair and held a strand of it.

"Give me a lock of your hair, Lemei."

"What?"

She burst out laughing.

"I want to have something of yours, to keep it on me at all times, wherever I go, so that you can be with me even when we're not together."

"But Balbius, a lock of my hair..."

"It's a token of love for us Romans."

"It's a funerary rite for us Gauls. And that scares me. I don't know if I can do something like that. And people will see it. My mother or my sisters will certainly notice."

"You'll find some excuse, I know you will. Please do it for me. I beg you."

The young woman hesitated but it seemed so important to him: she gave in.

"Alright, but not that much: half."

Balbius got up to fetch a big silver knife in the closet. She made fun of him: "Are you sure you don't need a sword?"

"Sorry, but I don't keep my sewing basket in my bedroom."

Lemei laughed at the effeminate pose he struck to amuse her. He took the opportunity to draw back the curtain on the window. It was still dark and quiet outside. You could only hear the sound of the toads in the garden pond. Balbius' room was the only one that opened directly outside. He had had the opening built, he said, so that he could enjoy the view on the aromatic garden and the orchard. But the main reason was that he wanted to be able to come and go at any hour of the night without having to pass through the atrium and the peristyle. His parents weren't fooled but had closed their eyes: after all, a young man needed to have some fun.

Delicately, Balbius cut off the lock of hair in the young woman's blond mane. She sighed when the tuft of hair fell on the bed and then smiled at her betrothed. She came closer for a kiss, one last kiss, knowing she must leave, but she didn't have the strength. Balbius held her very tight and what she took to be an expression of the passion they shared was in fact his way of putting an end to their time together. This was the last embrace, she had to go. He hated long drawn out partings: they kept him from his sleep and he was worn out. But, as they were embracing, Balbius suddenly let out a terrible cry. Lemei screamed with fright because he had started violently. She didn't have time to ask him what was going on: he fell back on the bed holding his foot. He was writhing with pain and howling. Lemei was struck by terror: "What's wrong, darling? What's wrong?"

"Something bit me; it hurts, by Hercules, it hurts."

His face had twisted in an agony of pain and beads of perspiration were running down his forehead. Then, his whole face turned red and he made only inarticulate sounds. Balbius' hands were clenched around his ankle and Lemei tried to pry them off. She managed finally and saw four very clear puncture wounds in the shape of a square from which oozed a trickle of blood. The entire area had turned purple. She still couldn't understand what could have happened to him. He wasn't howling anymore, but he was clutching wildly at the pillows, at Lemei's wrists, at everything within his reach.

And then, suddenly, the young woman saw a long black snake slither along the sheet and down the bed. It didn't look like any snake she had seen before: it was jet black, had a long, very slim and very shiny body and its head was crowned by a sort of horn. It was about to vanish under the bed but Lemei grasped Balbius' knife, jumped off the bed making sure to stay away from the snake, and, using the blade as if she were about to cut the neck of a chicken, sliced through the snake's body, right in the middle. The animal's last reflex was to turn back and bite his aggressor's arm. Lemei didn't pull away fast enough and the snake managed to strike at her forearm just below the elbow. The pain was excruciating. She gave a sharp cry: surely, now, whoever had still been asleep in the house, if anyone was, would wake up. But, before she even thought to flee or look at her arm, she was seized by an uncontrollable panic: what if there were more snakes, what if there was a whole nest of them all coming from under the bed! She jumped back on the bed with both feet and started kicking frantically at the pillows even though she trembled at the idea that each one might hide another snake, and each of her kicks could draw out another occupant. Finally, she lifted the sheet off the bed and flung it across the room.

Balbius had become stiff; his body was like a piece of wood struck by lightning. A white froth was bubbling on his lips and he seemed to be choking. Gurgling, rasping sounds issued from his throat and his nostrils. His eyes had turned into two white moons.

Lemei knew there was nothing she could do for him. She called his name and moaned. She didn't dare touch him and then the pain in her arm came back: she had to save her own life, she had to run away immediately. The Gallic sorcerer knew how to cure snake bites with sheep droppings cooked in wine. She prayed to find him at home! She mustn't waste any time. The snake had bitten her but the venom most probably had not had time to build up again after he'd struck Balbius. She could survive if she acted fast. She grabbed her clothes, slipped on her tunic summarily and darted off through the window, straight across the garden. As she ran madly away, the toads fell silent for an instant. The curtain had barely descended back over the window when the servants, armed with clubs and followed by Calidius Iassus holding his knight's sword, burst into Balbius' room, ready to fight the intruder.

All they could see in the room was Balbius, naked and still. His skin had already turned a grayish blue. His heart had ceased to beat but his body was so stiff that his heels were suspended above the sheets and his rigid neck held his head straight over the side of the bed.

XII

It was very hard to look at the corpse. Some people die well, they die peacefully; some people are granted the best death, in their sleep. Balbius Iassus had not been granted a good death: obviously, it had been brutal and painful.

All, around the body, looked solemn: Calidius Iassus was ashen. His son, his dear son, was lying there, dead. But Hadrianus Trevius was stricken as well since he had wanted to avoid any scandal after Cracius Vespasianus' killing and now had to face a second, most unwelcome, death; and Valerius Musa found no solace in being proved right in the previous instance. He knew that both deaths were necessarily linked and that his did not bode well for the city.

The doctor was holding up both sections of the black snake. This species didn't exist in Gaul; he had no name for this kind of snake. But Valerius recognized it: it was a rhinoceros viper. He had seen some in Gades, in southern Hispania when he was posted in the Betic province. The snakes were imported from the land of the Moors; they were prized for their aggressiveness and for their deadly venom and fetched a high price. There were no cures against their bite and death came swiftly, after a few minutes.

"There was nothing you could have done to save Balbius, even if you had arrived earlier," he told the doctor. The doctor turned to him and agreed:

"This type of snake is unknown in these parts, which means that it was brought here. And the fact that it was let loose in Balbius' room means that someone wanted to kill him."

Calidius Iassus' face had tightened once he realized the truth: his only son had been assassinated. He stood squarely in front of his son and looked at him as if he wanted to memorize the scene in every detail or as if he hoped that somehow Balbius would talk. Tears ran silently down his cheeks. Balbius, his son Balbius, was dead. He could hardly recognize him: his face was too contorted and, in death, his body had a greenish tint.

"What now, Hadrianus? This is the second death in two weeks. Shall we wait for the third one?" Tears were still streaming down his face but rage burst out in his voice. For now, the questions were directed at Hadrianus so Valerius let the first Magistrate answer them but he knew that they would soon turn to him and that he would be criticized, most probably because of his lack of results.

"Valerius Musa's investigations have not been very successful yet, but we will find the murderer."

"Someone in this city is killing our offspring, someone is targeting the sons of the Roman aristocracy. He's killed my son! And Cracius before him! He'll kill again if he's not stopped immediately. The city must be searched, he must be found. Or do you expect us to sit here and let ourselves be slaughtered like geese, by Juno! Valerius Musa!"

Calidius had turned toward the centurion as Valerius knew he would.

"What have you done since Cracius' death?"

"I have crisscrossed the countryside and searched every granary in the civitas."

It was increasingly difficult for Valerius to conceal what he really thought about the mission Hadrianus had given him.

"And what did you find?"

"Nothing. My orders were not to interrogate the friends of Cracius."

"So what? What's that got to do with the investigation?"

"Had I been able to question the people who knew him, the members of his family, the slaves and the servants of the family, I would have more to go on now…"

"What gall! Are you trying to suggest that the murderer is among our children?"

Calidius was outraged and so was Hadrianus. Valerius was really going too far. Still, the centurion refused to be cowed by their indignation and their anger.

"At this stage, I can't confirm anything but I can't exclude it either."

Hadrianus burst out: "How dare you…"

"Enough!" Hadrianus was cut short by a voice that had more authority than his. Everyone turned around, all equally surprised to see Quintus Vespasianus: he had been told of the tragedy and had come to Balbius' deathbed. His first words were for Calidius:

"I share your sorrow, Calidius, alas. I've come to pay my respects to your son."

Everyone was silent. Quintus' arrival reminded them of the decorum they should maintain in the presence of the dead man.

"Thank you Quintus. Thank you for coming."

Pain overwhelmed him again, tempering his desire for revenge.

"Leave Valerius out of this. This investigation is beyond his competence. The situation is too serious for us to attempt to solve it by ourselves. We must request a Propraetor from Tolosa or Burdigala to come as soon as possible. Meanwhile, we must organize ourselves and defend our children. I want us to hold a special closed door meeting of the council tomorrow morning to start working on this."

All the men who were standing around the corpse thought about this and then nodded their approval. Quintus was right.

"We are under the judicial administration of the Proconsul of Tolosa, we are still not under the jurisdiction of Burdigala," Hadrianus explained somewhat lamely since he was aware that, after events such as this, the whole affair would come out and the news would inevitably reach Augustus.

That spelled the end of his dreams of an imperial city with tax levies and a golden age for Lugdunum Convenarum. From now on, his name would be linked to a scandal; he would never manage to get back into the Emperor's good graces.

"Alright, let's send a messenger right now. We will meet tomorrow after the morning ablutions."

The servants had arrived. They were standing at the entrance to the room, waiting for the order to remove the body and start preparing it for burial. Calidius remained a little longer by his son's side and then turned to his wife and daughter who were crying together. He embraced them both and led them to their rooms. Now was the time for prayers and purification. As they were leaving, bent and knotted like a moving mass of pain, Calidius said over his shoulder: "Do what you have to do; take care of him now."

Quintus and Hadrianus followed; the doctor stayed to help the servants and Valerius took a little more time to finish searching the room: he looked under the bed and made a list of all the objects in the room when Balbius' body was discovered.

He also managed to examine the sheets very carefully and found a few whitish, almost transparent stains and some drops of damp blood.

As the women were moving the young man's body back in the middle of the bed, something caught his eye: a strand of long blond hair that was on the floor. It was very thin and could well have remained undetected on the golden flagstones. Undoubtedly, it belonged to a Gaul; there were very few Romans with such light colored hair. Knowing Balbius' tastes, it must have belonged to a woman. It had been cut with a knife, not pulled out. It was a straight and very precise cut and it could well have been made by the blade of the same knife.

"You did say that you heard a woman's cry, didn't you?"

The servant interrupted what she was doing and looked up at Valerius:

"Yes, centurion, a very sharp cry, right after master Balbius had screamed. And I'm not the only one; the men who came into the room with master Calidius also heard it."

"Are you sure it came from the bedroom?"

"Yes centurion, I'm sure. On this side of the house, the only room is Balbius' bedroom."

"And you didn't see anyone?"

"I got here after the men and there was no one. Master Balbius was just lying there, where you saw him and he was alone in the room."

Valerius walked over to the window, pulled back the curtain, and peered into the night.

"The garden, where does it lead to?"

"Nowhere. There's the wall and then the path that wraps around the grounds of the villa and leads back to the road to the lower city."

"What about the wall? How high is it?"

"Oh, I don't know...I'd say it comes up to here." The young woman was pointing to her chin.

"I see. Thank you."

Valerius returned to join the soldiers he had stationed at the entrance of the domus. Hadrianus and Quintus were waiting for him: they wanted the legionaries to escort them back home.

XIII

S erenia mea:
     I think that what I miss the most is the sun shining
over the Latium. Under the sun, everything seems acceptable,
even death. Here, people die young and are buried in the rain,
like Cracius Vespasianus. Maybe it will rain again when we bury
Balbius Iassus.

     Two young Roman men, barely older than our son, have
died; they were murdered. The murderer left no traces that we
can find. It's as if the gods wanted to tell us to leave this Gallic
land. Maybe Latins are not made to lord over these territories
so far from our Mediterranean sea.

     The distance from Rome is too great. I had the same
feeling when I was in Germania. Rome is eternal but the
Empire will not endure without its pines, its sun and its
glittering palaces.

     We think we are the occupiers here when in fact it is Gaul
that is holding us in thrall. We do take from its riches but we
give back far more than we get.

     We think we are the masters but what kind of master is he
who cannot do without his slave? To us these Gauls are ig-
norant barbarians, divided and vanquished, but in reality they

are proud and patient: they allow us to occupy their land only because they can benefit from our presence. They will suck us dry to the bone and, when there's nothing left, they will spit us out.

If they felt like wiping us out, they would kill us all just like poor Cracius and Balbius and we wouldn't be able to do a thing about it. So far from the homeland, we are powerless.

XIV

Tolosa: 55 miles.

Even though the carriage was fitted very comfortably, he was jolted in every direction especially when the driver had the bad idea, as he did now, of driving on the rough side of the road. Propraetor Rufus Riego leaned out of the window and shouted to the drivers: "Do you think driving on the bank side is amusing? Maybe you think it's too comfortable for me back here?"

"We are coming across many carts, Master: I can't stay in the middle."

In fact, an enormous load of marble blocks pulled by five oxen had just gone by.

"Get them to move out of the way! What is our escort doing?"

"It isn't always possible, Master. Some carts are too heavy to handle easily and ..."

The Propraetor wasn't listening anymore. He let the curtain that closed the opening and protected the passenger's privacy fall with an angry tug. Thirty four miles left to Lugdunum Convenarum. If everything went well, they would be there tomorrow afternoon.

These trips were always so tedious. This one was even more so. Traveling to Narbo took longer but at least it was more interesting. One could meet all sorts of people on the road and all sorts of vehicles: that road offered a sampling of the traffic coming from all over the empire, from Judea to Belgica; it carried an endless stream of wares and people of every nationality. Rufus Riego also knew the hidden inns where one could wager a little money without any risk of running into a patrol as one would in Tolosa where the law against gambling was strictly enforced. And of course, there were the pleasure houses along the way that made traveling a bit more agreeable.

The mission he had been given the day before, which was the reason he was traveling into Long-haired Gaul, was more like a penance. Granted, Lugdunum Convenarum wasn't very far from Tolosa, only three days' journey, but still, what tedium. Life in the provinces wasn't much fun but having to leave the civilized province of the Narbonensis and traveling deep into Aquitania was worse than anything. Not to mention that the via Domitia, the road that linked Tolosa and Narbo was much wider and in much better repair than this via rustica that ran along the Garonne towards the Pyrenees: the road had been hastily laid out and was most uncomfortable.

Tolosa: 56 miles.

Rufus Riego was wondering whether he should feel glad that they were getting nearer the city or whether he should deplore the fact that they were gradually leaving civilization behind.

They were fording a river: he could feel it from the way the front part of the coach dropped down first, followed by the back and he could hear the sound of the horses' hooves splashing in the water. He looked out the window to make sure that the rider in charge of the viaticum didn't keep for himself the coins he was supposed to cast into each river they crossed so as to ensure the protection of Mercury during the journey. The rider had stopped at the edge of the stream. He was busy fastening the purse to his belt and his horse had taken the

opportunity to drink. Rufus Riego almost regretted that he had
nothing to find fault with.

Sometimes when he traveled he would bring a few slaves
with him: a musician and one or two women to entertain him.
In any case, he never left without his cook. But, this time, the
Proconsul in Tolosa had asked him to leave for Lugdunum
Convenarum in all haste and he had had to rush to meet the
very short deadline he had been given and so he hadn't even
had time to pray to his family gods before leaving. He had
barely had time to pack a few belongings: everything fit into
just one wicker trunk. Therefore he was traveling light and
couldn't enjoy any of the amenities which usually helped him
relieve the tedium of the trip: neither wine, nor sex, nor fine
food, nor games. The only thing he could do was recline on the
soft cushions of the bed and rest until they arrived. But Rufus
Riego hated doing nothing. Even at night, in bed, he was
bored. That was the reason why he gave so many parties and
went out so much: he hated the moment when he had to lie
down and wait for sleep to come, to try and find sleep and
even beg sleep to come. He preferred to stay up as long as
possible until he was overcome by fatigue, work himself to
exhaustion and fall into a comatose slumber where life gave
way to death... as long as not a second of life had been lost.
The prospect of having to spend three days lying down without
doing a thing, as if night and day were just one long unin-
terrupted night, scared him stiff, literally. Lying down was fine
for sick people or invalids, not for the living. His mood, which
was never very light, now grew darker than night and he
needed a scapegoat: anyone would do; he just needed the
opportunity. The day before, he had ordered the convoy to
stop so he could reprimand a team of workers repairing a
bridge. There was a decurion with four of his men and three
Gauls who had been requisitioned. When the convoy reached
them, the three Gauls were taking a break and one of them was

drinking from a gourd. That had been enough for the Propraetor: before the coach had even come to complete halt, he had jumped out himself and started hurling insults and threats at the soldiers: they were a disgrace to the Roman army; it was criminal to let Gauls drink during work. He had refused to listen to the decurion who was trying to explain that what the Gaul was drinking was mostly water mixed with a little wine. Rufus kicked over the gourd and hit the workers. The legionaries were stunned by his violence and then dismayed when the Propraetor read their name tags, their signaculum, and noted them down. But this didn't surprise the men of the escort: their master was well known for his outbursts and in particular for his hatred of the Gauls.

During the rest of the trip he kept returning to the window and looking for the slightest incident that might provide some distraction.

But the sight of the never ending mass of trees, thousands, millions of them, of all kinds and sizes, didn't afford the least entertainment. On the contrary a feeling of ill will, as dark as the forest, kept growing in his heart. He hated the forests of Gaul and he hated the Gauls they spawned. He imagined them lurking in the shadows, ready to pounce on him. He should have taken the time to pray to his family gods; he should have consulted the gods before undertaking this journey. Easy enough for the Proconsul to send him off like that, but now he was here, in this coach, in the middle of nowhere with a measly eight man escort to protect him. He alone had to risk his life! These endless forests that rarely allowed any light were swarming with wild beasts and evil spirits. He wondered what kind of creatures, what kind of people could live under the dense foliage. How could they not be evil? And beyond the forests there were the cursed mountains that cut across the horizon! These mountains were not like the Alps with their high passes where the wind blew and the sky shined brightly.

The Pyrenees were more akin to an impassable wall: one could only circle around it or attempt to climb over it. Paths led down into darkening valleys and ended abruptly in an impasse. You had to crane your neck up to catch sight of the overhead pass and even mules could hardly make it through. Gaul was like these valleys: dark and brutish.

But he would show these Aquitanians – as they were now called – that Rome, even in the middle of the forest, held firmly in her hand the rod that would punish the criminals. In Rufus Riego's opinion the Gauls were just a collection of loose tribes who had only one thing in common: their unruliness. They were simply brutes who lacked any national sentiment and understood only one language: that of force. To call them "Aquitanians" on a par with the Roman colonizers who were settling these recently pacified regions was to give them too much of an honor. Of course, they all ended up becoming Romans as they had in the Narbonensis, but that could only happen after they had been forced into submission. They had to be tamed like wild bears and shown who was master.

He had little information regarding the circumstances surrounding the murders in Lugdunum Convenarum, which the city had called him to solve, but he was already convinced that the Convenes were implicated. There could be no other explanation. The Convenes had struck, just as the Volsques had done recently and before them the Allobroges and the Eduens. Wherever Rome had established herself, the natives had had to be brought to heel. Rufus did not believe in willing surrender. A nation that had not been broken would never completely give up hope of regaining its freedom: its people would always try and rid themselves of the occupier. He was aware that nowadays, in Rome, a different vision of Pax Romana prevailed and he was careful not to speak his mind in high circles. Still he was convinced that Augustus was on the wrong track: he should not be granting the Aquitanians so much freedom at such low cost.

Tolosa: 57 miles.

By Mercury and by Epona, what a life!

XV

Gallicus never took care of business himself. His Greek and Egyptian slaves, for which he had paid a high price, were extremely well trained in matters of commerce and did all that for him. He, in turn, rewarded them generously for their results. He promised them freedom if they contributed to his fortune and, since he always kept his promises, the slaves worked wholeheartedly toward that supreme honor, an honor that, for most slaves who belonged to other masters, remained an impossible dream. Most of his freed slaves actually remained in his service because working conditions were so exceptionally good and the amounts of money to be made from his flourishing business so attractive. Gallicus also enjoyed many political connections that reached far beyond Lugdunum Convenarum. His carts, laden with merchandise, crisscrossed the empire; he owned his own fleet of boats and a trading post in Ostia that enabled him to trade effectively all around the Mediterranean.

As Gallicus came in to meet him, Valerius Musa was keenly aware that he was disturbing a very powerful man.

Valerius suddenly felt very cold, as if all the marble that decorated the atrium stripped him of his clothes and was touching his skin. It made him realize how the austerity of the place created a space between the outside and the inside, shielding the house from the street and hiding the other part of the house, the part where there was warmth and color, and wall hangings, cushions and flowers. The centurion was not welcome: he was made to stand in the atrium, which was reserved for strangers, and understood that Gallicus had chosen to keep him there, in this inhospitable place, as an affront: he had no place here. He knew he would be allowed to ask one question and after that, whatever the answer, he would have to leave.

"What can I do for you, Valerius?"

"Thank you for receiving me, Gallicus Melala. I would like to speak to your son."

"Pomponius has nothing to say to you. He and I have already talked and there's nothing he knows that might help your inquiry. I'm sorry."

"Sometimes, in this type of matter, the least bit of information concerning the victim can help find the murderer. Pomponius was friends with Cracius and Balbius: his testimony can be useful."

"Usually, in this type of matter, as you say, a Propraetor investigates. And, as it happens, the Propraetor from Tolosa is arriving tomorrow. I suggest that you wait until he arrives before you trouble my son. He is in a state of shock: you would only add to his pain."

"I'm not acting on my own initiative. Hadrianus Trevius ordered me to continue the investigation while we wait for the Propraetor. We can't waste any more time. In any case, I am working for him; I have the same objective he does: to unmask the culprit. Time is running out, the assassin could be preparing his next crime. I beseech you, please, help me avoid a third victim. Let me talk to your son, just for a few moments."

Gallicus hesitated. Normally, he would have dismissed the centurion without ceremony; he would probably not even have let him into his house; but this time he was worried. Valerius could be right after all. Pomponius was hiding something, otherwise why would his son be avoiding him ever since Balbius' death? Why should he refuse to confide in him, when they had always been so close, so much like brothers? Pomponius had lost two of his best friends and yet he refused any comfort, he resisted every attempt on Gallicus' part to get him to talk about what had happened and relieve his pain.   It wasn't that he thought his son guilty or even implicated in the deaths but he felt certain that the boy did know something bigger than himself, something that terrified him and that linked him to the murders of Cracius and Balbius, something frightening enough that he would seek to keep it from his father.

Valerius was still standing in the atrium; he didn't dare move or make the slightest noise, sensing that it might trigger a categorical refusal. Gallicus, lost in his thoughts, was still blocking the entrance to the peristyle. He was speculating that his son might talk to the centurion, and, even though he couldn't stand the idea, he still didn't want to risk passing up a chance to help Pomponius in spite of himself.

"Fine, I agree. You can talk to him... but in my presence."

"Thank you, Gallicus."

Valerius had to wait a long time in Melala's office until finally Pomponius emerged from his apartment with his father.

The young man had changed: he was no longer the arrogant youth Valerius had questioned after Balbius' death. Gone were his arrogance and self confidence; he walked over to Valerius round shouldered, looking haggard, making vague gestures. The centurion sensed that this time he would be able to conduct a real interrogation and obtain real answers... if the young man's father let him do his work and did not interfere.

"My greetings, Pomponius."

Pomponius muttered some response.

"I know this is not the right time. You are in mourning and I'm truly sorry to bother you, but I need to gather as much information and as quickly as possible about your friends. You and Sennius and Lucius are the ones who knew Cracius and Balbius the best. I think you can help me."

Pomponius' lips trembled; his face flushed into a deep crimson as soon as Valerius began speaking to him; he avoided looking at the centurion. There was turmoil in his mind. Valerius was reminded of his impression as he was watching the young men at Cracius' funeral: this one looked like a small frightened animal. But what had seemed an air of barely perceptible, vague malaise had now, after the second death in the little group of friends, turned into absolute panic. This time, Pomponius knew he was hunted; the small frightened animal was being pursued by a merciless predator.

"I don't know anything more than what I told you before. I don't know who could have hated Cracius or Balbius to the point where..."

"I didn't come to talk about the murderer at this time. I want you to tell me what you know: tell me about you and your group of friends."

"What do you mean, our group? Who?"

"You five, you and your close friends."

"I ... I don't understand. What do you want me to tell you?"

"What do the five of you do when you spend time together?"

"I thought you wanted to talk to my son in order to find the murderer, Valerius. You won't find him among his friends."

Gallicus was sitting on the same couch with his son. He had positioned himself at the very edge of the couch, away from his son, but now, he moved closer to him. Valerius was annoyed because, in order to establish a dialog with the young man, it was vital that the father not interfere with their exchange.

"The group of friends is the target. I never believed that the murderer was among them but I am convinced that the next victim will be."

Gallicus swallowed hard: the blow had struck home. He knew, of course, that Pomponius could be directly threatened but no one had as yet said so in as many words and hearing it from the centurion's lips made the threat all the more real.

"If you are so sure, why don't you post two guards in front of my son's room?"

"I will, and I'll have Sennius and Lucius protected also. But I won't be able to keep them under protection for ever. I ask you, Gallicus: let me question him; it's for his sake."

Gallicus didn't answer. Valerius continued: "In order to understand who is after you, I need to know what you do when you're together."

"Nothing out of the ordinary. Nothing more than... Nothing more than what people our age do, I suppose."

"Still, tell me."

"We wrestle, we go to the baths, we ride our horses..."

"What about girls?"

"Girls?"

"You must have girlfriends; you do things with girls, things you talk about when you're together."

"Yes, well I mean, no...yes, but nothing much. We all think about it, that's for sure. We sometimes have a fling with a girl, but nothing serious."

Pomponius' lips had started trembling again and he began to fidget with his hands.

"Did Cracius and Balbius have love affairs recently?"

Pomponius gave his father an embarrassed look; Gallicus answered for him: "Cracius was to marry Staia Trevius; everyone knows that, including you, Valerius."

Valerius wondered if Pomponius' renewed agitation was caused by the presence of his father or whether there was something more. He sensed that now was the time to push harder but he knew he would better succeed if he managed to have Gallicus leave the room. He got up and took him aside: "Would you mind leaving us alone together, your son and me, Gallicus? He might feel more comfortable talking about these things in your absence. You understand what I mean?"

He gave him a knowing smile and added: "You know how these things are; we've all been young and it's not easy to confide in one's parents in matters of love."

Gallicus didn't really like being asked to leave. He distrusted Valerius; for a simple centurion, he was taking many liberties. But he had to admit that the man was convincing.

"My only concern is your son's safety."

Gallicus thought about it and made up his mind: "Alright, I'll go."

Before leaving, he laid his hand on his son's shoulder and looked at him for a moment silently urging him to tell the truth.

The centurion returned to his seat but pushed it closer to where the young man was sitting, looking helpless now that he was alone with Valerius. They were now face to face: Valerius was right in front of him, very close and looked squarely into Pomponius' eyes. The young man couldn't escape him anymore. His confusion was growing.

"So, what about at night, what do you do at night?"

"What do you mean? We sleep at night, of course."

"Enough, Pomponius!"

The young man was startled. The centurion's tone had been sharp but he had not spoken very loudly. Still, he looked beyond Pomponius' shoulder to check that Gallicus hadn't been alerted by the outburst. He no longer spoke in the respectful tone expected of a plebeian addressing a nobleman; he spoke with the authority of a magistrate about to uncover the first real lead in his investigation.

"There's a killer out there who is intent on eliminating all of you, one by one. He has shown what he's capable of by killing twice. Believe me: he'll kill again if we don't find out who he is."

Pomponius was trembling even more.

"One of your friends died slowly, his body was emptied of its blood; the other suffered excruciating pain: would you like to guess how the third one will die? What I told your father is true: even having permanent protection won't prevent the murderer from finding a way to get to you."

Valerius had found the right words: Pomponius' weak defense began to crumble. He couldn't hold out any longer and gave in completely: all of a sudden, tears, big childish tears, long contained, were gushing out from within, streaming down his face. That didn't stop Valerius, on the contrary: "The only way to keep you safe is to arrest the murderer and for that to happen you have to tell me what you have done and, most important, to whom."

"Nothing, we did nothing, I swear."

Pomponius seemed to crumple. Still crying, doubled up over his knees, he screamed, barely lifting his head up: "We didn't do anything bad."

"What do you mean, 'nothing bad'? What did you do? Say it, by Mercury!"

He took hold of Pomponius by the arm and shook him violently.

"Speak or you'll die, you fool. Do you really think keeping a secret is more important than denouncing a murderer? Each time, it happened at night; tell me who was with Balbius the night he died. And Cracius, where was he coming from when he was killed?"

"The long-haired ones, the long-haired girls!"

Pomponius screamed into the cushion he was clenching on his knees. Valerius couldn't make out what he was saying.

"What? The what?"

The young man's face was contorted with pain, his eyes were red and his mouth slavered. He said again: "The long-haired girls, that's what we call them."

Valerius pulled back a little. Pomponius was shaking spasmodically and the centurion put his hands on his shoulders; he patted the young man's back in a gesture of affection, then stood up and sighed with relief. Finally, he had a lead; he knew all along that they had been hiding something from him. He looked up and saw Gallicus Melala in the entrance to the corridor through which he had left: he had actually been standing there and had heard everything. Both men looked at each other. Gallicus shook his head in silence.

XVI

"I hope you had a pleasant journey, Rufus Riego. We are honored to receive an imperial Popraetor. Welcome."

"Salve, Hadrianus Trevius, thank you for putting me up at your house. I'm exhausted. What an endless journey, by Minerva. And what a terrible road!"

A slave was on his knees under the running board of the coach to help Rufus Riego step down. Others were busy unloading his chest and taking the horses to the stables where they would be rubbed down and where the coach would be parked.

"Would you like to eat something? I had the pistor dulciarius prepare some sweet cakes: his oven cake, his erneum, is a delight."

"No, later. I'm dying to take a bath first."

"Of course. I've had water brought from the thermal baths of Lixon by the barrel. You'll see: it's wonderfully soothing after a long trip. People say it's almost as good as the water from the thermae in Neapolis."

"Most important is my back: it hurts. Send me a masseur to start."

Hadrianus snapped his fingers in the direction of his man-servant, Eutrapelus:

"Tell Canius to prepare the baths for our guest. Tell him to get my massaging oils."

Hadrianus guided Rufus Riego to the center of the peristyle where two slaves stood waiting:

"Solemnis and Neva will show you to your apartments. They will take care of you during your stay. Ask whatever you wish: their only wish is to make you comfortable. I'll see you again after your ablutions and we'll discuss the matter that brings you to Lugdunum Convenarum."

"Good. Meanwhile, tell the centurion in charge of the garrison to come here. I want to talk to him."

"Valerius Musa?"

"Yes. He's the one who is investigating, isn't he?"

"Certainly, but do you really want to talk to him tonight? Don't you want to rest first?"

"I don't intend to linger in this place. So I don't want to waste any time. Have him come and call a meeting of the quattuorvirate for tomorrow morning at the first hour. We will meet in the curia but behind closed doors. Thank you for putting me up, Hadrianus; I'll see you later at dinner."

Rufus was still being massaged when Valerius reported to his apartment. The centurion was accustomed to sharing the baths and the changing rooms with his men but he was a little nonplussed at being confronted with a Propraetor in the nude wearing only a towel over his privates. The man's small, plump, not very well proportioned body and his pale skin was at odds with the idea Valerius had formed in his mind of this very powerful and reputedly pitiless man.

The centurion's arrival put an end to Canius' services. Rufus sent the masseur and the attendants away so he could be alone with Valerius. Hadrianus was outraged at being kept away, in his own house. He was suspicious: he saw the hand of

Rome in this. He wondered to what extent Rufus Riego might
have been instructed to take advantage of this sorry business to
eliminate him or, at the very least, to use it to bolster the case
against him among Augustus friends who would all be too
pleased to see him ruined: a fitting end to an unfinished affair.
Hadrianus had forgotten all this but intrigue breeds paranoia
and old reflexes are quick to return.

Still, he put up a good front when the two men returned
after more than an hour together, and he warmly returned the
centurion's salute. After the soldier left both magistrates went
in to join Hadrianus's wife for the evening meal. Hadrianus of
course would not broach the subject directly during the cena
but he did attempt to find out what the two men had discussed. But, in spite of devious attempts to prompt him, the
Propraetor wasn't fooled, and Hadrianus quickly gave up and
figured that if Rufus Riego wasn't forthcoming, he would be
free later on to ask Valerius and learn all that he wished to
know.

XVII

"How many young Gallic women did this purported "contest" involve?"

Hadrianus had yet to ask a single question. Valerius, as he was recounting what he had learned since the beginning of the investigation, was starting to relax; now, he straightened up slightly and assumed a more soldierly attitude as he faced the assembly composed of the city's magistrates and the Propraetor. Lorus Divolus was also present. This time, though, he wasn't there just to listen to the debates as he usually did; this time the Propraetor had charged him with writing down everything regarding the investigation that would henceforth be said. As a manager he had been given all kinds of administrative work, in every possible sphere but now he found himself, for the first time, in the role of scribe in the course of the proceedings of an imperial investigation. He had rarely felt so excited.

"Twenty in all. Cracius was ahead, if I may say so. He had managed to lure seven of them into his bed to Balbius' five. Pomponius and Sennius had scored three each; Lucius was last with only two. It was easy to corroborate Pomponius' declaration because of the locks of hair that he and his friends would take from each girl and bring back to the others as proof. Without a lock of hair there was no win."

"So, you found twenty locks of hair."

"No, only nineteen. I didn't find the lock of hair from Cracius' last catch."

"What surprises me is that you didn't find these tufts of hair sooner. Didn't you search the young men's rooms?"

Rufus Riego had, in fact, directed the question more at the quattuorvirate than at Valerius.

"I didn't. I wasn't authorized to do that."

As he said this, Valerius had turned toward Hadrianus. The Magistrate understood that this little scene, this game of question and answer had been set up by the Propraetor and the centurion in order to confound him. That was what they had been plotting the night before during their interminable conversation. He pretended not to understand the point and shrugged his shoulders.

"In any case, why would the number of girls involved be important? Nineteen, twenty, twenty one: what's the difference?"

"What is important to me is not the number but the names of these girls. And, as it happens, last night, Valerius Musa, whose excellent investigation I wish to commend, gave me the names of the young women who were part of the list of their conquests. Pomponius, Sennius and Lucius gave them to him, each separately, and their lists corresponded exactly."

The Propraetor pulled out a roll from the sleeve of his toga. Calidius Iassus jumped up; he couldn't resist asking:

"Have you got the name of the girl who was in my son's bedroom when he... when he..."

He couldn't finish the sentence. His son's funeral had taken place the day before; the same pain and exhaustion showed on his face that before him had crushed Quintus and Apronia. He had insisted on being present at the meeting called by the Propraetor because it had always been a point of honor for him to fulfill his duties as the third magistrate of the city, but the effort he had to make to avoid breaking down was almost too much for him.

"No, Balbius had not told his friends about this assignation. We still don't know who was with him that night but we will find out. We will explain his death. The answer to this question is here!"

Rufus held up the roll with the list of names:

"Because of course, the reason for these deaths is revenge. The father or the brother or the fiancé of one of the girls whose name is written here most certainly wanted Cracius and Balbius to pay for the affront they have perpetuated on their females. Gauls don't fool around with such matters, do they, Gedemo?"

The Gaul had remained silent until then, as had Caius Retus and Calidius Iassus, the second and third magistrates. As for Lorus, he was absolutely forbidden to say anything. He wrote, he kept quiet, but listened intently to every word that was being said.

The atmosphere was heavy. Never, since the creation of the civitas had the members of the council been so close to reigniting a war between the two peoples. The Romans and the Convenes had even begun to live in good harmony, and Gedemo, their chief, was well regarded by his magistrate colleagues. The four men at the head of the city had been working together for several years and the three Roman magistrates had come to value the qualities of their Gallic counterpart. They acknowledged his willingness to work for the good of Rome and his ability to unite his people around him. That Rufus Riego should call him out in such an offhand and almost provocative manner embarrassed them.

Gedemo still did not react but the other magistrates, knowing him well, sensed his fury.

Rufus rolled up the parchment and brandished it like a weapon. He looked at Gedemo with an ironic smile. The Gaul's silence, which Rufus interpreted as a sign of weakness, hid a far deeper turmoil. Gedemo measured the import of the accusations wielded by the Propraetor from Tolosa: he was inferring that the murderer was a Gaul, and if that proved to be so, the Convenes as a whole would be disgraced. Everything he had been working to achieve, the sacrifices he had made, the years he had spent convincing his people to cooperate, the settlements he had reached with the Romans, his efforts at putting an end to the internal strife between the Convene tribes and at supplanting the other powerful families, all that would be threatened. Everything he had done in the hope of securing a future for himself and his people within the empire would come to nothing.

The ruination of all his efforts as the leader of his people was not the only thing he dreaded: as a father, he was gripped by an even greater fear. These young Roman aristocrats had evidently managed to lure more than one innocent girl into their arms with dreams of a brilliant future. They must have promised love but also a richer, more exciting life than the prospect of marrying the son of an allied family from the small Gallic nobility. His daughter had been promised to just such a young man since she was a girl. He had to admit that even though Epotsorovida had never challenged her father's decision, she had never shown much enthusiasm for her future spouse, Dorix, the son of Diviciacos. She was his daughter; he had always loved her and trusted her but why should she be more virtuous or less naïve than the others? What if she too had been seduced? The very thought that his daughter could have been involved with one of the five young Romans drove him mad.

"What's wrong, Gedemo? Have you lost your tongue? Maybe you're thinking of your own daughter? Maybe you're thinking that she might very well be on that list, aren't you?"

Gedemo would not stoop to this man: he didn't ask if she was. He was caught between a feeling of humiliation and the impulse to stand up and fight for his honor. He could kill if he found out that his daughter had lost her honor. He remained silent.

"Please, Rufus, we have always been a united quattuorvirate and we need to remain united if we want to find the assassin."

"A united quattuorvirate? To me, you are a triumvirate with a fourth leg that was added out of plain demagoguery. I don't see how you are going to preserve this so called unity when a Gaul is running around killing the young Romans of this city."

"Gedemo is our friend. He is the chief of the Convenes and has been a magistrate of the civitas ever since its founding. Let us not treat him in this way, please."

"Not treat him this way?"

Rufus Riego had shouted. He stood up and shouted again:

"Not treat him this way! When, in fact, he might be a suspect in the case I am charged with investigating on behalf of the quattuorvirate of which he is a member!"

"You are going too far, Propraetor. I can answer for Gedemo; we have complete trust in him, he could not be implicated in…"

"You can answer for him, can you? Would you still answer for him if I told you that his daughter was Cracius' last mistress?"

The four magistrates were stunned.

Gedemo jumped up and Rufus instinctively recoiled. The Gaul was much taller than he was; he wore his traditional garb, his hair was long and his beard abundant. He was no longer young but still very impressive: his powerful chest seemed about to burst into a battle cry. He looked as if he was about to hurl himself at Rufus' flabby body. But instead, Gedemo turned to Valerius, his face trembling with rage:

"Valerius? Valerius?"

He was imploring him to say it wasn't true, that all this was nothing but a horrible plot, a trap set against him.

The centurion looked at him sadly:

"I'm very sorry, Gedemo. The three young men all say the same thing. The day before his death, Cracius told them he was going to spend the night with her in her father's house on the road to Burdigala."

Gedemo didn't reply. He stood very straight, his legs set slightly apart, his fists tight. The only noise was that of Lorus' stylus on the paper. The centurion was ready to intervene if Gedemo made the slightest threatening move against the Propraetor.

The tension was now at its highest. Everyone knew what the Gallic chief must be feeling and they feared that he wouldn't be able to contain himself any longer. Hadrianus made an attempt to deflect some of the tension: he turned to Valerius, hoping to give Gedemo time to regain his composure.

"Why didn't you tell us earlier?"

"Lucius and Sennius only confirmed it two days ago. I knew what this meant and so I decided to wait until Rufus Riego was here to tell him directly."

"And you did well, centurion. It was high time that I should arrive and it was high time that this investigation became more objective."

"What do you mean, Rufus? The quattuorvirate called on you of its own accord and did so quickly; we acted as we should have. If you have something to reproach us with, please explain yourself."

"The Quattuorvirate asked for my help because Quintus Vespasianus demanded it: you had tried to pass off the first murder as an accident. Now we discover that the daughter of one of the members of the Quattuorvirate slept with the first victim on the night he was assassinated. What I am saying is that it is time that this investigation be taken out of your hands because all of you here are interested parties. Do I make myself clear?"

This was a slap in the face for Hadrianus. Lorus couldn't believe his ears, but he was present, and he heard those words. Caius and Calidius also had never heard anyone speak like that to the First Magistrate.

Valerius added:

"Since I knew Pomponius, Lucius and Sennius were most probably the killer's next targets, I asked them not to leave their apartments and I put two guards day and night in front of their bedrooms. They're safe."

Hadrianus was livid to think that he hadn't even been informed of all this.

Gedemo was still standing, with the same attitude; his body was tense with burning rage. He was totally indifferent to the battle that was being played out between Hadrianus, Valerius and the Propraetor. Suddenly, without a word, he ran down the couple of steps from the platform; Rufus, thinking he was going to attack him, ducked. But Gedemo didn't even look at him: he passed by him, crossed the council room and then disappeared in the direction of the lower city.

The heavy wooden doors slammed shut and, inside, the high walls echoed with the sound and heightened the councilors' unease. None of them had any idea what to say or do. Calidius and Caius, who had not gotten involved in the discussion until then, now wondered which position they should take: defend Gedemo? Protest against the way Rufus Riego mistreated Hadrianus? Both things seemed dangerous since it was clear that the Propraetor had intended to crush the Gaul and compromise the First Magistrate. They were afraid of associating themselves with Hadrianus in his fall from grace.

Valerius was particularly displeased: he had been the one to report the events of the past three weeks. He had been obliged to explain to Rufus why his investigation had not included the Roman aristocracy; he had been obliged to reveal Hadrianus' reticence. Now he felt torn between his feeling of satisfaction that the investigation was finally going somewhere and his skepticism about the Propraetor's brutal methods. In Hadrianus' mind, it was clear that the centurion had betrayed him. He should have known that Valerius would stab him in the back. He had never trusted that narrow minded soldier who probably envied him his fortune and thought he had finally found an opportunity to rise above his station.

He thinks he's found the way to revive his faltering career. Maybe he's naïve enough to think that by disparaging me he'll get good marks from the provincial administration and reap some benefit. That lousy bastard, that son of a bitch!

Hadrianus glared at Valerius with hatred. He would make him pay for this betrayal.

The centurion saw that look and knew very well what Hadrianus was thinking. He knew what it would cost him, a plebeian, to have compromised an honestior, a member of the Roman elite, but he also knew what he would have to pay if he ever kept the facts from Rufus Riego. There had already been two victims in a case he was in charge of and he wasn't going to let Hadrianus turn him into a scapegoat for his own ill advised decisions. In the end he had chosen to bite the hand that fed him rather than the one that held the rod.

"You see: not a word of explanation; he just runs off to his people. Is that the mark of a magistrate?"

Rufus seemed to enjoy attacking Gedemo. Nobody said anything. Only Caius Retus, who was looking at the door, thought out loud:

"I wouldn't like to be his daughter. Gedemo is an upright man but he is not known for his leniency, and, as you just said, Rufus, the Gauls don't take their daughters' virtue lightly."

"Who cares? Let him beat her and lock her up if he wishes to; that won't make a bit of difference. He's the one who will end up behind bars very soon."

"What do you mean? I don't understand."

"The murderer is there, in the low city, among the Gauls: that's where we will find him. I will have all the men who belong to the families of the girls on the list arrested."

"What?"

"Gedemo included. He'll be the first, as a matter of fact."

"What!"

It was like a clap of thunder in the curia. Hadrianus and Caius stood up in a vain attempt to protest this madness but Rufus went on speaking as if he hadn't noticed them.

"We will make them talk. The murderer is among them. We shall find him and make him confess. It's as simple as that."

The three Roman magistrates were stunned. Valerius also was visibly taken aback. Even Lorus wondered whether he should write this down. The Propaetor went on as if thinking out loud, for himself:

"From the beginning, I had an idea that this had to be the work of the Gauls."

"But having them all arrested! You can't do such a thing!"

"We must stanch the bleeding. I cannot let a killer bleed our young one after the other."

He sat down, readjusted his toga and looked at the three magistrates:

"Sit down, he said to Hadrianus and Caius. We are in a meeting of the quattuorvirate here, not in a salon."

They obliged, thinking, again, just how insulting the Propraetor's tone was. Hadrianus thought he would quickly have to find a way of getting rid of him.

"Arresting them en masse will be very badly perceived by the Gauls. They will consider this an affront on our part."

"We will tell them that it's the only way we can arrest the culprit and that those who are innocent will be quickly released. After all, that may be the best way to secure their help in unmasking the killer. They must be made to understand where their interests lie: either they go on living like animals and protecting criminals or they take part in our imperial effort. Valerius, how many men do you have in the garrison?"

"A maniple: less than two hundred legionaries."

"That's more than enough to isolate the lower city. When the time is ripe, you will post a man in sight all around the Gallic sector of Lugdunum Convenarum with orders to forbid anyone from entering or leaving the perimeter."

"Propraetor, with all due respect, two centuries well never be enough if the Gauls decide to rebel."

"I've thought of that. This morning at dawn I sent a messenger to Tolosa to ask for immediate reinforcements. They should get here in five days of forced marches. We will wait for their arrival before we make a move."

Caius Retus was the oldest among them. He made another attempt, hoping to sound like a wise elder: "Rufus, please reconsider. We don't even know whether the murderer is in fact a Gaul. You risk creating bloodshed in the civitas for nothing. This is a very dangerous idea."

"Caius is right, Propraetor. The gods know that I, more than anyone else here, want the assassin to be punished. That is the only thing that counts for me now. We must protect Sennius, Lucius and Pomponius and keep them from the tragic fate that befell my son, but we should not create panic in the entire city; I don't want us to reopen the old wounds that existed between us and the Convenes."

Caius patted his old friend on the shoulder and turned again to Rufus:

"Keep the young men confined and under surveillance, but for the rest, exercise caution. Let Valerius finish his investigation under your supervision and then we will decide what action should be taken according to what you have found out."

The Propraetor wasn't convinced by Calidius any more than he had been by Caius.

"When I conduct an investigation, I expect results even if I have to use force. In some cases it's necessary."

Hadrianus was dismayed:

"Do you understand the consequences of what you intend to do? You are going to destroy years of working together toward peace. Our civitas is an example for all of Aquitania; you don't realize the long term consequences of a show of force, and not just here in Lugdunum Convenarum, but also across the entire province."

"Lugdunum Convenarum an example for all of Aquitania? I certainly hope not, or else it's an example of how to fail! A city that allows the sons of the Roman aristocracy to be killed one by one with impunity! Believe me. You are blinded by your feelings of friendship for them: the only thing Gauls understand is force. We cannot show any weakness, we must crack down and put a stop to this crime wave immediately."

"I beg you to consider the consequences before you act. You arrived here only yesterday evening; you have heard only Valerius and, already, you are about to make decisions that threaten the fragile peace we have achieved here…"

"As for that, I must say you are right, Hadrianus."

Hadrianus didn't conceal his surprise. Was Rufus mocking him or had he really changed his mind? He didn't know what to think of the Propraetor.

"I'm going to hear the testimony of Pomponius, Sennius and Lucius. These three must finally explain what they were doing and they must be made to face their responsibility. Have them summoned immediately! Valerius, have them brought here now."

Hadrianus, Caius and Calidius looked at each other doubtfully. Valerius hesitated and the Propraetor repeated his orders:

"Go, centurion. As for us, let us go for a walk."

He got up and walked toward the door:

"You too Lorus. Take your stylus and your rolls and come with us."

They were all taken aback and wondered what this sudden turn of events could mean. But, since the Propraetor was walking out the door without waiting for them, they got up and followed him.

When Rufus came out on the square, the patrol in charge of his protection immediately formed into two columns on either side of the group of magistrates. Odors of spira cakes and bread being baked wafted up from the merchants' neighborhood. Today there was no market so the forum was relatively empty. Only the stalls selling cloth and jewelry, which had a permanent concession, attracted a few early clients but, otherwise, the city was not completely awake.

"I'm terribly hungry. Hadrianus, show me around the shops in your good city."

Rufus Riego walked around like a self satisfied conqueror seemingly unaware of the dire mood his words had created among his companions. His attitude seemed unreal. He behaved in the leisurely manner of a person come to take the waters who was discovering the spa at which he would spend the summer. He pretended to have forgotten that he was about to launch a massive offensive against half the population. As he walked by the taberna medica of a doctor, he stopped to ask the clinicus, who was busy setting out his unguents and drugs, what he could recommend against migraine, from which he had been suffering for many years.

He kept repeating: "I'm starving."

They continued their walk, still protected by the double column of the patrol, toward the fountain where dried fruit and pickled vegetables, ham and cheese, were for sale. Hadrianus had told Rufus about his plans for the development of the city and the Propraetor asked how the new sewer system would work. At first, the merchants and their clients eyed the marching soldiers and the magistrates with apprehension. Then, they became less suspicious when they saw this apparently important man – judging by his clothes and his bearing – engage in small talk with them and ask questions about their wares. They answered his questions with a short yes or no but then quickly became more talkative when he asked them about their professions. They went on and on, interminably: one said he raised snails that were just as good as the snails of Illyria; another explained how one should coat plump dormice with honey. Every one, in the end, said how proud they were to welcome these worthy visitors into their shops.

"Augustus was right: you can keep the people quiet with enough food and games. But I think that isn't all it takes: you have to flatter them a little too," Rufus whispered into Hadrianus' ear.

As for the first magistrate and his two colleagues, their feeling of unease was growing. They had not forgotten that this strange and unseemly little walk was intended to kill time while they were waiting. Rufus was engaged in a very serious investigation and yet he treated the magistrates in the most offhand manner, as if they were themselves lowly merchants.

After he had eaten and decided he had had enough of this bit of entertainment, the Propraetor ordered the squad to turn back and they returned together to the curia where Valerius was waiting with the three young men. The centurion and his soldiers had roused them out of bed in all haste, without any explanation other than that they were acting on the orders of the Propraetor from Tolosa. Their fathers, Gallicus Melala, Eutrapelus Senica and Faustus Sorandis Basseus, worried and outraged in equal manner, had come with them. They knew Rufus Riego's reputation, which was why they had decided to come and make a show of their displeasure at their sons being rounded up like criminals.

When the magistrates walked into the large room, the three young friends and their fathers were standing in the center, at the foot of the platform. They had instinctively picked the spot where the light fell from one of the openings, to stand in the warmth of the sun's rays. They turned suddenly toward the entrance, their faces showing their anxiety. The three fathers walked up to their friends Hadrianus, Caius and Calidius and asked what was going on.

The place gave off a disagreeable impression of cold emptiness. That was exactly the setting Rufus wanted. He didn't give Hadrianus time to answer. He came over himself to greet them, but perfunctorily, with the barest show of respect for their rank. Then he climbed on the platform.

"Now, young men…"

He took his time settling in the chair usually reserved for Hadrianus and waited until the magistrates were themselves seated. With a wave of his hand, he invited the three fathers to sit on the councilors' benches, turned toward Lorus to make sure he was ready to take notes and, with his blue gaze, looked the three boys in the eyes, one after the other.

"I am Rufus Riego Pompeius, Propraetor of Tolosa; I'm acting on the direct orders of the Emperor in Rome."

He spoke slowly, with long pauses between each sentence. Each word was intended as a blow to the three young men. Rufus was entirely in command and knew the impact his words would have. His introduction had evidently been calculated very precisely to give him the upper hand over his interlocutors from the start.

"I have the right of life and death over every slave, freedman, Gaul or Roman citizen, across the entire senatorial and imperial territory between Narbo and here. My decisions are final; only Augustus can rescind an order I have given. Do you understand?"

The young men were too terrified to answer but Gallicus Melala was already beginning to fret.

Rufus resorted once again to one of his favorite means of striking terror into the hearts of those under his authority: after a few soft words spoken as if by a friend, he followed up with brutal invective and ominous threats.

"You understand fully?"

This time Pomponius, Sennius and Lucius had to acknowledge his words. They answered in unison: "Yes, Propraetor Rufus Riego."

"Good."

"I protest. Rufus, this is no way to talk to our sons."

"We are in a tribunal here, Gallicus. We are not in one of your warehouses; you can speak when I give you your turn."

"This is a disgrace! I'll report you to the prefect of Narbo. Your methods are shameful. Wasn't it enough to drag our sons here under military escort without any warning?"

"I'm afraid I just don't have the time to observe the niceties of protocol. If two young men hadn't died and if other lives were not in danger, I might perhaps have sent you an invitation by courier. But I must act swiftly. I'm sure you will understand that I am acting in the interest of your own son."

Gallicus was somewhat placated but he still didn't give up completely:

"I thank you for coming all the way to Lugdunum Convenarum, Rufus Riego. We appreciate your help, but, as you yourself rightly said, our three sons are in danger; they are victims. Two of their best friends have died, they are in a state of shock and they're frightened. In spite of all this they agreed to collaborate and they told Valerius everything they know. I can't see why you talk to them in a way I thought was reserved for convicted criminals."

"Precisely because they are guilty!"

Hadrianus was beginning to tire of the Propraetor's tricks of oratory. Calidius and Iassus also didn't bother to react. But the fathers made a great show of indignation: how could their sons be put on the spot in such a way? They found the Propraetor's repeated provocations harder and harder to bear and they vowed to complain to the authorities. Lorus had stopped writing and held his stylus up, waiting for Rufus to proceed. The Proparetor continued unperturbed:

"They are guilty of having brought the civitas to the edge of civil war. Who else is responsible for this pathetic competition and its outcome, the deaths of Cracius and Balbius?"

"But…"

"Quiet, young man. You will speak when you are asked to do so."

Lucius lowered his head.

"In any case, what could you say to justify your participation in this affair?"

"Cracius was the one who drew us into this competition. He was very successful with the girls; he thought it was fun to do that."

"Cracius bears part of the responsibility, it's obvious. But he is dead. Balbius and he payed a sufficiently high price; they should be left in peace now, but not you. You, in the end, are the only ones left to answer for what happened. Not to mention your culpable silence after Cracius' death: had you told the truth then Balbius' death could have been avoided."

"But Balbius himself told us not to talk about the long haired ones, not even to our parents. He even threatened us."

"It's true, Propraetor. He said Cracius should never have slept with Gedemo's daughter, that going with the daughter of a chief was sacrilegious. He said that if we revealed the facts we would be exposed and we would become living targets for the Gauls…"

"So, basically, you're not guilty of any wrongdoing in this affair. All you did was follow Cracius and keep quiet when Balbius told you to. Not only did you behave like fools, you didn't even act on your own initiative."

His hand under his chin, he seemed to ponder over something. He gave the three young men a silent contemptuous look.

"The killer struck the brave ones among you: you are just a pitiful bunch of cowards, alive but cowards."

"Watch your words, Rufus," Hadrianus cut in.

"Hadrianus, I weighed every word I said."

The curia fell silent. A sparrow had flown into the building and couldn't find its way back out. It kept chirping and flapping its wings in a panic up against the ceiling. It mistook the rays of light projected unto the walls for openings and threw itself desperately against the brightly lit stones, directly opposite the exits, thinking he would escape into the sunny springtime sky. Lorus, not having to write yet, took the opportunity to look up and followed the bird's desperate flight. Each time it attempted to escape through the trompe l'oeil, the bird hits its head harder against the wall.

Both generations of Melalae, Bassei and Senicae, were silent, the fathers sitting on their benches, the sons standing facing the Propraetor. They had now fully accepted their role as the accused and were waiting for the verdict.

Either for rhetorical effect or because he was really taking time to think things over, Rufus was also silent. He stroked the hollow in his chin just below his lips with the index of the left hand and then put it under his nose to smell the odor of his own skin. This was one of his habits when he thought; Lorus had noticed it.

The bird had knocked itself senseless and was lying at the foot of the wall. Lorus returned to his tablets.

"Why 'the long-haired ones'?"

Lucius, Pomponius and Sennius didn't understand the question.

"Why did you use that expression, 'the long-haired ones'?"

Sennius answered:

"This region is called Long-haired Gaul, so, just for fun, we called Gallic girls 'Long-haired'. When we were small, we thought our parents used that expression because the Gauls who lived here had lots of hair. We thought it was funny and we joked about it later and then we started calling the girls in the city the "Long-haired ones".

"Is that the reason you keep a lock of hair from each of your conquests?"

The three boys didn't deny it.

"I suppose that too was one of Cracius' ideas."

They hung their heads and didn't answer. They didn't need to: Rufus had figured them out completely.

"How long had this competition been going on?"

"A year, maybe more: a year and a half."

Rufus Riego nodded. He wanted to get to the bottom of the whole matter; he wouldn't skip any question.

"And yet, Gallic girls prize their virginity very highly. How did you manage to convince them to sleep with you? Did you force them?"

"No, never! They all consented. We promised them marriage; we told them we loved them. You know… we did what men do when they want to get a woman. We didn't do anything wrong."

"Not all Roman aristocrats copulate with Gallic girls. I imagine these young women didn't enjoy being abandoned once you had deflowered them. You never had a problem with any of them before Cracius' death? You were never threatened?"

Sennius, feeling very much ashamed and trying to avoid his father's eyes, confessed in a very low voice:

"We knew they wouldn't dare say anything… They had lost their virginity, they had been bad. They would be rejected by their families if they revealed what they had done. So all they could do was… They just had to keep quiet."

"But, by Venus, how long did you think this little game could go on before one of the girls' families found out and the scandal erupted?"

Sennius was the one who answered again; this time, he was practically crying.

"We didn't really think about any of that. We were just having fun. It's so boring here in Lugdunum Convenarum. It's so far away from everything. What else could we do?"

"Stop moaning. You're a disgrace to your class!"

Rufus spoke these words in his usual cutting tone. Then he switched to the practiced eloquence of the prosecutor summing up the charges against the accused.

"You are the aristocracy of Rome, you are the Empire's elite. Your birth gives you rights and advantages and you enjoy them to the fullest. But you also have duties: you must be an example. When you coupled with these Gallic girls you sullied your honor and blackened your families' name. Now, because of your carelessness the entire city is at risk of being drawn into a political crisis. You have put all the Romans in the civitas in danger. For this, you must be punished."

"We understand, Propraetor."

Only Sennius had spoken but Pomponius and Lucius had nodded in assent.

"Since you are bored here in Lugdunum Convenarum and since you don't know how to spend the time of day, you will be put in the service of the Empire. Augustus has just created a new corps of civil servants to establish a census of all the peoples in the Empire and to draw up cadastral maps of all its territories in every province. He is looking for educated men who know how to write and how to count. You are just what he needs. You will work for this corps for two years. After that you may return to Rome and find a wife but you will forever be persona non grata in Lugdunum Convenarum. Do you understand?"

"Yes Propraetor."

This time, the three young men had answered in unison. Their fathers knew there was nothing they could do or say. They were rich influential men and each one had contacts in high places but their sons' guilt had been established beyond a doubt and their transgression was too serious for the sentence to be overturned. It was, after all, a fairly lenient form of punishment.

"I trust that you are aware that I am acting in your interest. We don't really know how the Gauls are going to react in the coming days when they find out what kind of a game you have been playing with their daughters, and it is for your own safety that you should leave this region without delay."

'Yes Propraetor."

"You may go now. Tomorrow, at this hour, I want you to be gone."

Rufus signaled with his hand that the meeting was over and that there was nothing more to be said. Lorus knew he was done with his note taking. The hearing had ended. He would have much to tell Stella when he got home at noon.

The three Roman worthies went up to their sons. They felt like hitting them and embracing them at the same time, both to reprimand them and to hug them. Maybe, had they been stricter, had they brought them up more frugally and not like rich parvenus free to do as they pleased, maybe the young men would not have been so careless, maybe they would not have behaved like idle decadent fools. Maybe it was a bad idea to have brought them here to live. Had they stayed in Rome, things would certainly have turned out differently. For one thing, they could have fornicated with whomever they wished without igniting a second Gallic war.

The young men thanked the Gods for being alive but this hasty departure and the prospect of having to leave their families and friends and having to forsake the comforts of their domus for a most certainly uncomfortable life in the service of the Empire filled them with bitterness.

They walked out of the curia and across the forum together with their fathers and their retainers.

Hadrianus watched them go, all six of them: he knew what they were feeling, part sadness, part relief. He thought of his own daughter. She was the same age, she was among their friends; he could imagine how he would feel had she been the one who had to leave so quickly and in such circumstances.

Lorus approached to remind him that they were to go and see the representative of the stone cutters' corporation about some unpaid bills. Hadrianus answered that they would take care of that later; he was far too worried about what was being hatched to take care of ordinary business just then. Lorus asked if his services were needed. Hadrianus said no and dismissed him. He had only one thought: he must find a way to thwart the Propraetor's plans at all costs, and find a way to prevent Gedemo's arrest.

The two magistrates, Caius Retus and Calidius Iassus, also left the curia. Caius held his friend by the arm. The proceedings of that morning had been an ordeal for Calidius: he felt weak and heartbroken as he left the forum. Rufus Riego, however strong his authority and however rough his manner, could never bring back his son.

A sedan chair awaited Hadrianus and Rufus. The Propraetor was still talking with the centurion:

"In the days to come, before the reinforcements arrive, I want us to prepare the Gauls' interrogation. I want to find out everything there is to know about each of the men we are going to arrest. Hadrianus, as First Magistrate, is certainly the one who knows the people of the civitas the best, but I was told you also have good relations with them. I think your help will be very valuable to us, Valerius."

"I'll be honored to help you, Propraetor."

"We will be meeting this afternoon, after the bath, in Hadrianus' house. Be there."

"Yes sir."

Valerius Musa saluted; the Propraetor's personal escort left at a run toward the upper city. The centurion gathered his men and ordered them to march back to the fort. He was thinking about the amazing events of that morning. The investigation was out his hands; he had known it would happen: it was in the nature of things. But the Propraetor had never disowned him; he trusted him. It was something he could be proud of. Still, he had many doubts. He knew that the decision to arrest all the men in the girls' families was mad…and wildly unfair. He didn't just feel puzzled by this: he was faced with a real dilemma. He had built excellent ties with the Convenes; the Propraetor intended to use them, but, his methods being what they were, the relations between Romans and Gauls were bound to deteriorate in the days to come. He would become the instrument of repression, something he disapproved of. How could he regain the Convenes' trust when the Propraetor, after wreaking havoc in the city, would finally leave? He knew Rufus would do anything in order to get results; he was prepared to raze the entire Gallic neighborhood if necessary to find the murderer. Valerius agreed with Hadrianus on at least one thing: Rufus Riego was going to create an irreparable breach between the inhabitants of the civitas.

He was frightened by such an outcome. He couldn't explain why. After all, he was only a soldier; it wasn't his job to enter into such considerations. Since the Propraetor, appointed by the Emperor himself, had decided that such measures were necessary, all he should do was obey and not have any second thoughts. Eventually, the relations with the Convenes would go back to normal, or they would take a different course. Should he care?

Couldn't he accept, or at least, be content with such a thought?

If only they had proof that a Gaul had committed those crimes. But, here too, he had doubts.

He reached the camp: Canius and Flaccus would surely be waiting for him and, like the night before, after his interview with Rufus, they would ask him to repeat what was said, and tell them if there was any progress in the investigation, whether they had a lead...

Like the night before, he would answer that he wasn't authorized to say anything and that he only knew what the Propraetor would let him to know. He would tell them that just as Rufus had congratulated him the night before for the way he kept his logbook, so this time he had praised him for the way he had conducted the interrogations. And just like last night they would make fun of him; they would say that he was showing off. They would give him a friendly shove and say: "Come on, tell us."

Just like last night.

XVIII

My dear Serenia:
          Lightning strikes the tree that stands outside the forest, not the tree that hides in the middle of all the others.

Maybe that's my problem: I can't stay safely in the middle; I always need to step outside the ranks; I need to take a step back and get a good look at the forest.

That's when I run the risk of being struck by lightning. The Propraetor has arrived from Tolosa and he has brought a piece of the Empire with him. I had forgotten, and everyone including Hadrianus had forgotten, what Rome's authority truly feels like. Like lightning, it is quick, accurate and pitiless. We were reminded that we are Romans, occupiers, not Gauls trying to live peacefully with the indigenous peoples.

Very soon, I'm going to have to go back and hide in the forest.

I no longer doubt our capacity to conquer and occupy. But our methods are so violent that I doubt that the price being paid by these people is worth it. I see more clearly now why it is that Rome reigns over the entire known world. It conquers of course, but it does more than that. Once it controls a territory, however far it might be, Rome knows better than any empire how to throw out its tentacles. First it sends its soldiers, then its tradesmen and finally its administrators. It crushes, charms and holds.

And then sometimes, the settlers forget to hold the people down and chaos ensues. Rome does not approve of that. In those cases it sends Propraetors to punish the weak settlers and the unruly Gauls and it sends in the troops if necessary. That is why Rufus Riego has come to restore order in Lugdunum Convenarum.

Young Romans have been hunting down Gallic girls to pass the time.

Someone is killing the Romans, one by one. So now, Rufus Riego is hunting down the killer.

XIX

Valerius Musa had returned late from his appointment at Hadrianus' house. After work, Hadrianus and Rufus had invited him to stay for the cena. Lucius and Julius, Hadrianus' sons had come to pay their respects to their father's guests. The Propraetor had asked the usual questions and they had answered politely. "Are you behaving in school?" "Do you want to become soldiers one day like our good Emperor?" They smiled secretly at Valerius whom they knew and liked and then they vanished when they were ordered to. Claudia ate with them but went to bed right after the dessert, when the men began discussing city business. It was the first time Valerius had shared a meal with the honestiores. He had never before eaten such delicate fare served in such beautiful plates. He had never seen such a profusion of dishes, sauces and sweet wines.

Now he understood why aristocrats were so plump. The dining room itself was more beautifully decorated than a consul's villa. He couldn't believe his eyes. The murals represented the gods crushing the Titans and armies doing battle. Their stories were unfolding on the walls. In each little recess of every scene Valerius discovered some new and intriguing detail to gaze at.

What turned his attention away from the murals was the
flute player who came in at the end of the meal. He kept time
with castanets fastened on his feet and from time to time he
stopped playing to recite some beautiful poem. Valerius rarely
had any opportunity to hear music apart from military ceremonies or during religious rites and he found the melodic
sounds of the musician's instrument entrancing.

Hadrianus' daughter was not present during the meal. Still,
at one point during the evening, Hadrianus sent for her so that
she would accompany the musicians. She entered the dining
room, curtsied respectfully, sat at the harp, took time to tune it
with the musician's panpipes and played some melodies her
father requested. Everyone sat entranced and surprised by that
delightful girl. Later, when she had returned to her rooms after
wishing them a pleasant evening, the deep sadness in the way
she played lingered on among the men. It was as if sadness
itself had touched the chords of the harp instead of her delicate
fingers. She had never turned to look at the diners and she
never smiled.

Claudia found her daughter's melancholy annoying. She
could understand that the death of Cracius would make her
grieve but that mood had become a habit and her daughter
wallowed in it. It had been going on for several months now
and Claudia was fed up. Hadrianus, on the contrary, saw the
mark of a great sensibility in such melancholy: it impressed him
and convinced him that his daughter was special. The fact was
that her momentary presence had touched every one of them;
it had plunged Valerius into a mood he had never experienced
before, bringing him close to tears. He had had a lot to drink
during the meal. And now as he was alone on his camp bunk it
felt as though it were rocking like a skiff caught in a gale un-
leashed by Neptune himself.

A little while earlier, about to go to bed, he had felt like
masturbating. He almost regretted having declined Hadrianus'

offer of one of his slaves or one of the boys in his service, whoever he preferred, to spend the night with. Valerius had seen the look in the woman's eyes: one of fear and disgust. He didn't like making love that way.

Now his bunk was rocking too much indeed. Staia's image haunted him. But she wasn't playing the harp; she was looking at him and seemed to want to tell him something, something urgent. Her lips moved but she made no sound because what she wanted to convey couldn't be said.

He chased her from his mind. While he continued to manhandle his penis, pulling back the slightly creased foreskin, he tried to imagine all the things he could have done with the slave he had refused: she had an enormous buttocks which he would have enjoyed penetrating violently. But as he conjured up this scene he was involuntarily reminded of Serenia who disliked being taken from behind – she used to say she wasn't a mare; then, just as he had successfully managed to get hard, his wife's disapproving eyes blighted the scene and spoiled the pleasure that was about to come. Finally, his imagination dried up, he abandoned the attempt and tried to go to sleep even though the bunk was still rocking.

Rufus Riego had no such qualms. He had always been honest with his wife Vicentia: she knew he would always attempt to seduce anything that could be seduced. In return, he had never interfered with her sexual appetites, whatever they were. Often he had to acknowledge that she was more insatiable than he was; she consumed sex like food, at times because she was hungry for it, or she had nothing else to do; at other times because she craved it like a sweet or it helped her fight off melancholy; at the very least, it kept her warm or she just needed a change.

He was in the expert hands of the two slaves Hadrianus had placed at his service, Solemmnis and Neva, two Egyptian women that had been bought from Julius of Iserna in Rome.

They had entered Claudia's service and her friends admired their great beauty and their gentle touch so typical of women of the Orient. The warm glow of their skin, its tones of nutmeg and licorice, gave their arms and faces such a fluid and perfectly smooth surface, that all their movements seemed softer. Egyptian women were highly prized for their deep knowledge of massage and healing and the Trevii were proud to introduce their guests to the delights of their art.

Rufus was enjoying them fully. Hadrianus had also sent him one of his male slaves. Not that he was personally attracted to masculine charms but watching another couple make love stimulated him. Rufus watched the Egyptian girl's body jolt with each thrust of the young man's loins. The Propraetor, meanwhile, let the second girl take care of him. She had swallowed his penis deep into her mouth, stopping from time to time to rub it against her breasts or under her armpits: this Rufus found unusually delightful. Never in his fairly long life of debauchery had he experienced this practice: a kind of fake coitus that felt so real in the wet tenderness of the slave's skin. Rufus Riego was so delighted that he began to think that these few days in Long-haired Gaul were not going to be so awful after all. Hadrianus Trevius' hospitality and his kitchen were more than honorable, considering how far removed the civitas was from everything; his slaves were relatively refined and quite devoted. Lucius, Pomponius and Sennius being safely taken care of, he might be able to take advantage of the welcome he was being given for the next few days. But all the attention that was being lavished on him would not deter him from the mission he had been given by the Proconsul in Tolosa: to deal with the utmost severity with the First Magistrate of Lugdunum Convenarum. No one, in the higher circles of power, had forgotten his past opposition, as senator, to Augustus' rise. Obviously, Hadrianus Trevius had a guilty conscience: this lavish reception betrayed his anxiety. Of course, the deaths of the two young Romans were very embarrassing for him. The least he could do was to make the Propraetor's stay as pleasant as possible. But what he really held against the magistrate were not the murders for which he could in no way be held responsible, but his lax handling of the civitas and particularly the empathy he suspected him of harboring for the Gauls. Rufus had witnessed that attitude during the first day of his stay. It was clear that his fecklessness and empathy had brought about the present situation: his relations with Gedemo were so ill defined and ambiguous that they prevented him from acting decisively against him now, and toward the Convenes as a whole. Hadrianus was no longer a magistrate, he was no longer the authoritarian father of the city who leads and punishes if necessary; he had become everybody's friend, a generous, forgiving grandfather, well liked by everyone, certainly, but someone you could take advantage of.

These would be the highlights of the report Rufus would write for the Proconsul; it was among his prerogatives and, even though the investigation of the double murders was the primary object of his mission, he had been given to understand that observing Hadrianus' actions and reporting on them were another of its most important aspects. Hadrianus would have to confront the situation he had created in the civitas; he would have to realize how wrong he had been and remedy the situation, or else...

Eumachia Melala had not finished her shellfish. She was reclining opposite her son and gazing at him lovingly.

"I beg of you, Pomponius, promise me you'll be careful. You don't need to distinguish yourself; don't be too zealous. If one these Gauls refuses to cooperate, don't put yourself forward!"

"Come on mother, all I'll be doing is taking a census; I'm not going off to conquer Britania. Plus, I'll be accompanied by soldiers. I will never be acting alone."

"Stop worrying, Eumachia. Our son will be safer there than he would have been here. When I think of what happened to…"

"Stop! Do you want to bring bad luck to our house? Don't talk about these horrible things."

"The auspices are clear: tomorrow is a lucky day for traveling. Pomponius has nothing to fear apart from the anger of the gods, but he hasn't offended them at all: those Gallic girls were just…"

"Not one more word about that, Gallicus, I beg you."

As she said this, Eumachia frowned at her son, scolding him ever so slightly before she smiled a forgiving smile; had there not been the deaths of Balbius and Cracius, after all, those little peccadilloes wouldn't have had such bad consequences. Pomponius took a second helping of oysters: he knew he wouldn't be eating like this for a long time. His father had ordered a real feast prepared in honor of his son's departure. Gallicus was secretly rather pleased that Pomponius had to start his career far away from home, in the service of the empire. The experience would strengthen his character. At his son's age, he had served under Julius Caesar in the conquest of Gaul. A military campaign transforms a man and Rome had had no dearth of battles to offer its young men at the time. That was how one became a knight or a senator. The punishment meted out to Pomponius and his friends would be beneficial to them: what had led them into this adventure was their completely idle life; were it not for the tragic deaths of the two young men, the whole thing would have been, to his mind, just silly. Gallicus thought that a dose of administrative rigor would turn Pomponius into a more responsible person and that when he returned he would have matured and would be better prepared to play his role in the family business. As for now, Gallicus would not have entrusted him with a shipment of olives; he was really hoping he would be able to count on him upon his return from his "service".

Sennius Basseus was kneeling before the altar to the family gods. His parents, who professed to be very pious and virtuous, insisted that the meal be frugal and the evening spent in prayer and sacrifices. The only relief they allowed were farewell visits from the wives and daughters of their friends. Prima Retus, the Second Magistrate's wife, and her sister Julia brought wine and honey; Claudia Trevius and her daughter Staia offered sweets for the journey. Normally, the Vespasiani and the Bassei would also have come to wish the young man a favorable journey but they were in mourning and their presence would have been improper. In any case, a feeling of unease now kept the families apart: they all shared the same feeling that Cracius and Balbius alone had paid for a mistake all five boys had engaged in together. The bitterness and despair that the Vespasiani and the Iassii felt at having lost their sons opposed them to the other parents who were secretly relieved that their sons had been spared by the gods in their wrath.

Such was the feeling in the Senica family: they had sent the slave in charge of ritual in all haste to the neighborhood market to buy a bull for the sacrifice. He was told to buy the best animal he could find and he had brought back a bull weighing at least fifteen hundred pounds. With the cooks he had bled it in the atrium. A slave girl, a virgin, had washed Lucius' hands in the blood collected in a gold vase and then the family had eaten the animal's liver and heart; the bull itself would then be carved up by the scissor and the carptor to be distributed according to tradition to the less fortunate among the Roman citizens.

Lucius' parents had decided not to ask him any questions, not to mention the Gallic girls or his two dead friends for fear of provoking the gods and casting the evil eye on their son.

Hadrianus waited up until he felt sure that he had heard the end of the love making in Rufus' room. It was very late when he finally slipped out of bed, but, as he was leaving his room, he came across one of the two Egyptian women: the Propraetor had sent her to fetch some wine. He asked her what state his guest was in by then and how much energy and appetite he still had for the women. She assured him the Propraetor was sated and that he just wanted a last cup of wine before going to sleep. He waited while she returned to the bedroom and heard Rufus' voice for another few minutes. Then there was complete silence, he thought, and, walking on tip toe, eluding even the ostiarius asleep in the front hall, Hadrianus, wearing a rough cloak of dark cotton, left the house. In his hand he held a papyrus roll; he hurried off in the direction of the lower city.

XX

"What do you want, Hadrianus?"

Even though it was very late Hadrianus apparently had not interrupted anyone's sleep in Gedemo's house. The chief's house was larger than traditional Gallic houses; it was more comfortable; it was the house of a chief and the walls were made of dry stone instead of raw mud.

It had become customary for rich Gauls to use Roman construction materials and Roman building methods but Gedemo was against that. A chief was duty bound to preserve the traditions of his people. His house had no fountain; there were no terra cotta flagstones, no sheathing on the walls, no paintings.

Hadrianus always felt repulsed when he visited this house. Everything in it put him off: the dirt floor, the feeble light produced by a few torches, the smell of fat emanating from them, the rustic wooden furniture; he couldn't believe he was on an official visit to a Gallic dignitary. He was aware that the size of the house and its very relative comfort, at least when compared to most of the houses in the lower city, was an expression of great wealth, still, he could hardly imagine living in any worse conditions.

"Good night Gedemo. Please excuse this late visit. I had to talk to you."

"If you are here on behalf of your Propraetor, you shouldn't have bothered. I have nothing to say."

"Rufus Riego does not know I am here; my visit must remain a secret."

The Gaul looked over to his wife to indicate that the men needed to be by themselves.

"Forgive me Gedemo, I don't want to offend your sons, but I must speak to you alone."

The three young men didn't budge. They stood proudly with their arms crossed on their naked chests and looked straight at him.

"Leave us," their father commanded.

They silently left through a small opening in the wall opposite the entrance where Hadrianus still stood. The door was so low that they had to stoop. The two men were standing in the main room that functioned as a dining room, an office, a reception hall, and was the main space where the family lived. Hadrianus supposed that behind the mud wall there were bedrooms and a kitchen.

He still hadn't been invited to sit. Gedemo looked at him for a while.

"What is it you want to talk about with me considering I'm a suspect in your imperial investigation?"

"Those accusations are ridiculous of course."

"Still, you didn't come to my defense this morning."

"I'm terribly sorry for what happened this morning in the curia. I hope you know that you have the full support of the Quattuorvirate. But what could we do? I was hearing the facts for the first time just like you."

There were a few seconds of strained silence and then Hadrianus asked:

"Did you talk to your daughter? How is she?"

"I no longer have a daughter."

Gedemo said these words in such a cold tone that Hadrianus was filled with dread. Fearing what he might hear, he didn't dare ask him what he had done to her.

"I did not kill her if that's what you are thinking. Contrary to what your Propraetor says, Gauls are not savages. Epotsorovida was branded by iron and cast out of the city: such is the ancestral law of the Convenes. She is condemned to wander and live alone."

"The three young men, Lucius, Sennius and Pomponius have also been ordered to leave the city; they must be gone by morning."

"Well, as you see, we execute our sentences more swiftly. My heart will bleed as long as I live but all the fathers of the other girls on the infamous list will do as I did, when the names are revealed."

"That's what I came to talk about. We can still avoid the worst."

"The worst has already happened: our daughters have lost their honor and, whatever you say, my sense is that you are powerless now. Obviously you are no longer the one who decides in this city."

"You're wrong Gedemo, the worst is still to come. Rufus Riego is convinced the murderer is a Gaul. It's hard to disagree with him: everything points to your people. But what you don't yet know and what I've come to tell you is that he is preparing to have every man in these girls' families arrested. Each and every one of them!"

Gedemo, who sat in his great ceremonial chair decorated with boars' heads, gripped the armrests:

"He's mad. And you? You will let him do that?"

"I have no choice Gedemo; his authority extends over the magistrates of a civitas."

"That's exactly what I was saying: you no longer are in charge in your own city. In any case, as far as I'm concerned, I won't let him do that. My men will take up arms if we have to."

"Reinforcements are on their way from Tolosa, an entire cohort, enough to crush any rebellion. You'll be slaughtered if you revolt. The fact is that you and your sons are at the top of the list. He's going to throw you in jail, Gedemo."

If Hadrianus had not come in person to warn him of the Propraetor's senseless plan, Gedemo wouldn't have believed a word. Ever since that morning's humiliation in the curia, he had been brooding over what to do and veering between fury and cold reason. Part of him wanted to answer the call of honor, and revolt in defiance of the Propraetor and slit the throats of the three dogs who hadn't yet been killed; but he knew that if he refused to submit and his men took up arms it would be a death sentence for his entire people. The Propraetor would seize the opportunity to send in the troops and raze the Gallic city, thereby eradicating the Convene people for ever. Gedemo had sensed Rufus Riego's visceral hatred and disgust for his people. He had never felt that hatred before, not in the Roman soldiers he had fought against when he was young and his people were still free and not in any of the settlers who had come to Lugdunum Convenarum. He felt this hatred now but couldn't understand where it came from and he was aware that there was nothing he could do to fight it.

Hadrianus was aware of the conflict raging in Gedemo's mind: as the Fourth Magistrate of the civitas, he was moved by his conscience but, as a Gallic chief, he was bound by the most profound and ancestral feelings of honor. Hadrianus looked at the coat of arms of Gedemo's clan that adorned the ceremonial shield on the wall: it depicted a wild boar and a stag stopped in flight by the hunter's arrow. There was a troubling resemblance between that stag and the old Gallic chief: the same stunned surprise, the same incomprehension in their eyes.

"He can't do that. He hasn't got the right. I am a chief and a magistrate."

"That won't stop him. He'll do anything to find a culprit but he won't move before the reinforcements arrive in Lugdunum Convenarum. The best way to avoid this arrest is to hand over the person who killed Cracius and Balbius."

"But how do you want me to…? I haven't the faintest idea who that could be."

"You are the chief, Gedemo. Use your power; call a meeting of the families, gather all your men and make them talk. You have four days to find a culprit."

"I will not let you humiliate my people, Hadrianus."

"Gedemo, believe me, I want to avoid that at all costs. That's the reason I'm here tonight. I'm taking enormous risks by coming here to warn you. If it were known…"

"I've always been loyal, Hadrianus. We had an agreement: I kept the Convenes in check. You never had reason to complain. In return you promised us peace and prosperity. Now is the time for you to prove that you can keep your end of the bargain."

"Keep your voice down! No one must know I'm here."

Instead Gedemo stood up and shouted:

"I will not let the Romans besmirch the honor of my people; I will not let them flout my authority and discredit me; I will fight back."

"Be quiet, you fool. Do you want the whole city to hear you?"

"I'm warning you Hadrianus, if Rufus Riego targets my people, you will regret it too."

"What are you saying? Are you threatening me? You have nothing to reproach me either: it's thanks to me that you are sitting in this chair, thanks to me that you were elevated to the rank of magistrate. Don't forget that it is thanks to me that the Convenes are masters over this entire region of Aquitania. I

came here tonight as a friend, to help you, and this is the way
you treat me!"

Gedemo's sons had burst into the room. They surrounded
their father and stood facing the magistrate. Lutarios, who
seemed to be the fiercest of the three, pointed his powerful
arm at him and barked:

"Don't speak like that to my father, Roman, or I'll make
you eat your words."

"Quiet, Lutarios. Do not be disrespectful to the First
Magistrate of the city."

His son took a step back but went on staring at Hadrianus
who reflected once again on the likeness he had seen between
Gedemo and the stag on the shield: Lutarios was certainly
more like the wild boar.

"We are not friends, Hadrianus. We never were. We are
barely allies and you are going to do what allies are supposed to
do: you are going to suffer the same fate we do. We shared the
good days, now we will have to share the bad ones."

Hadrianus no longer controlled the discussion. He couldn't
believe that eight years of trust and collaboration wouldn't survive the first test.

"Listen Gedemo, try to calm down. Yes, Romans have
taken advantage of some young women among your people,
but two were murdered and the other three are banished. That
is a heavy price to pay. Rufus will not be content with the
status quo. The man who murdered Cracius and Balbius must
be brought to justice. In all probability, one of yours must have
sought revenge."

"Whoever did this killed to avenge his daughter's honor. I
would have done the same had I known earlier that Cracius
had slept with my daughter. That's the way things are done
among my people!"

"The Vespasiani and the Iassi will not rest until they have
the culprit. A life must be taken; that's the way things are done

among the Romans. All I'm asking you to do is to help calm things down, to hand over the murderer to the Propraetor before he himself comes here to get him. That way, the investigation will end, your authority won't be questioned and peace will be restored between our two people; it will be best for everyone, believe me."

This time, Hadrianus had struck home. Gedemo calmed down, he listened and was now pondering the magistrate's words.

"What happens if I can't find the killer in four days?"

"I'm not asking you to hand over the culprit; I'm asking you to find a culprit. Sometimes the good shepherd has to sacrifice a lamb in order to save the flock."

Gedemo acquiesced. He turned to his elder son, Bellovese, who was also the wisest of his children and would someday succeed him. He looked at him, asking for his approval and then said:

"Alright, I will deliver a culprit to Rufus Riego. This is a great sacrifice you are asking me to make, Hadrianus. I hope you won't forget it."

"You are acting in your own interest."

"And you in yours."

"That isn't so. Now that Cracius is dead, I can no longer take advantage of what had been for me and my family an extremely favorable alliance. And who is responsible for this? One of your people: don't forget that either. Here!"

He handed him the papyrus he was holding.

"This is the list of the twenty girls: Rufus is going to look for the murderer among their families. Find someone in any of those twenty families and hand him over before the reinforcements arrive on the fourth day before the Ides of May."

Gedemo took the list. Hadrianus nodded goodbye, and left, without waiting for an answer.

Outside, the moonless night shielded him from prying eyes but it also made his progress difficult. The streets in the lower city were littered with garbage of every sort and with broken pottery shards; he stumbled over drunks. He couldn't wait to get home and take a soothing bath to wash away all that filth.

XXI

Lorus Divolus gulped down his beans. He was thinking of something else. He always ate breakfast alone, after his wife and children. As he dug into the mashed beans, he thought again about the discovery that had been preoccupying him since the night before: the Propraetor had, in effect, seized power over the city. Without really knowing how it had happened or exactly why it had happened, he sensed that this was something momentous, something he could take advantage of. For the first time, he had seen Hadrianus' authority as First Magistrate challenged. For the first time someone had brought down this all-powerful man whom he had always thought of as being incapable of the slightest weakness.

Everything had happened very fast. First Cracius died, then Balbius, then the Propraetor had arrived; then suspicion and discredit had fallen on Gedemo's people, then Valerius put Hadrianus on the spot and Rufus had disavowed the First Magistrate... The last four weeks had been so eventful, it was all somewhat bewildering.

The important thing is to be cautious, he thought. Under no circumstance would he rush into anything.

"Tell me, father."

"What?"

"You were smiling. What's so funny, tell me."

Lorus Divolus looked at his younger daughter who had slipped her head under his arm and kept him from bringing his spoon to his mouth. She looked up at him.

"Nothing, Lepidina. I was thinking."

"About what?"

"Nothing. It's not for little girls."

She understood she should stop bothering him and she ran off to bother her brothers instead. Lorus could hear them fighting for a while but he was so used to it that he didn't pay any attention. Even his wife singing while she did the dishes couldn't interrupt his thinking.

Some things were going to change. Hadrianus might not remain at the head of the civitas forever; now might be the right time for Lorus to emerge from obscurity and finally assert himself. He sensed that, with Rufus Riego, everything was possible. If he managed to gain his trust and let him see what a good manager and overseer he was, he might be able to benefit from his master's fall from grace. As things stood, he felt he had already made a good impression on the Propraetor.

For now, he must go on doing what he had been doing for the past three days: simply wait. He knew that nothing would happen before the arrival of the troops: they were expected, if all went well, on the fourth day before the Ides of May, two days hence. Like everyone else in the curia who had heard Rufus declare that he had sent for reinforcements he was both fearful and hopeful but, mostly, impatient. It was high time they identified and punished the culprit; sending in a cohort from Tolosa would not go unnoticed. The rumor that the troops were arriving had quickly made the rounds in the city: first the news was met with puzzlement and curiosity but people were worried now.

"It's very bad for business", said Vettius Gracilis. He had come that morning to see Lorus because he wanted him to convince Hadrianus to call a meeting of the council and inform all the different guilds of what was really going on. Some of his clients had postponed their orders under the pretext that they wanted to know what was really happening in Lugdunum Convenarum before they invested in the city. Some merchants were even talking of moving to another city where being Roman and being alive were not two incompatible propositions, where it was possible to be Roman, rich and alive.

"Don't be ridiculous. The merchants and craftsmen of Lugdunum Convenarum are not in any danger."

"If that's the case, why did they send for a Propraetor? And why the troops? They're not telling us the truth. Why don't they tell us what's going on?"

Lorus walked back to the entrance of his house, looked up and down the street, to make sure no one had seen the head of the merchants' guild enter his house. As overseer of the city's business he had certain prerogatives but he was not allowed to meet with people such as Vettius in his own home and without informing Hadrianus. If the First Magistrate found out, he might think Lorus was plotting something behind his back.

Outside, there was nothing but the warm early summer sun. It wasn't nine yet and the light drew a sharp divide in the middle of the main street that ran from the baths up to the oppidum: it lit the houses that faced east while the opposite side of the street remained in darkness.

"Why don't you go directly to Hadrianus?"

"He's more remote than ever, you know that. He spends all his time with that Propraetor. He listens to you. Talk to him. Convince him!"

"I'll see what I can do, but in the meantime tell the members of your guild and the other councilors not to worry. They aren't directly affected by all this."

"All this", as you say; we would certainly like to know more about "all this."

"We will, once the troops get here. But until then, if you want to talk to me, please come to my office in the forum, don't come to my house again."

Lorus had finished his meal. He always took a nap afterwards, when he had time, and today, he had plenty of time. Hadrianus had not only suspended all daily business, he also put on hold many of the city's projects and so Lorus had a lot of time on his hands; usually, at this time of year his municipal duties kept him very busy. So he lay down on his bed and hoped that Stella would join him: he knew he couldn't find sleep because of everything that was on his mind. To attract his wife's attention, he coughed but she didn't hear him so he coughed again, louder this time and the three children laughed because they knew very well what these signals, that their parents exchanged when they felt like sex, actually meant.

An hour later Lorus was sleeping so soundly that he didn't hear the two horses galloping up the street to the fort, their hooves clattering on the cobblestones. There was only one rider; he was leading the other horse by the reins. He was a messenger sent by the centurion commanding the cohort that was still two days' forced march away. The messenger had probably been riding without stopping, switching from horse to horse as each became tired. It was obvious from the exhausted horses and the rider thundering up the street that the news he was bearing had to be very urgent.

As he entered the courtyard at the fort, he jumped off his horse before the groom even had time to grab the reins and asked to speak immediately to centurion Valerius Musa. The legionaries on guard escorted him to the officers' quarters. The messenger was surprised: centurions normally slept in a tent along with the other high ranking officers. His legs felt numb and his back was aching and bruised, still he thought the two soldiers walked too slowly: it seemed to him as if the whole garrison was moving in slow motion and had lost any sense of urgency. Had they known what news he was bearing they would have moved a lot faster.

A few minutes later, Valerius appeared. He obviously thought there was an emergency: he bounded out of the fort and ran toward Hadrianus' house, the rider in tow walking stiffly and trying to keep up with the centurion.

Valerius entered the house and asked to speak to the Propraetor: he knew he would find him here since Rufus rarely left his host's comfortable home. The centurion was out of breath and his uniform was hastily fastened. The ostiarius understood that things were serious and let the two soldiers enter without announcing them first to the master and lady of the house. He led them to the atrium and asked them to wait. As the minutes went by, Valerius could barely stand it. The messenger, now that his mission was accomplished felt less concerned: he sat down to rest on a window ledge. He quickly stood at attention when he heard the rustling of linen togas; he couldn't see the faces of the Propraetor and the senator because the sun was shining in his eyes.

"What's going on, Valerius?"

Hadrianus had asked the question but Valerius spoke to the Propraetor which once again upset the magistrate.

"Forgive our intrusion: we have some very bad news."

He turned to the messenger:

"Speak, legionary!"

"Salve, Propraetor Rufus Riego."

The young soldier, with sweat still trickling down his face, hit his chest smartly with his fist and extended his arm in a salute to the two honestiores.

"My name is Lucilius Apolinarius, legionary, 3rd maniple, 5th cohort of the Claudia Pia Victrix legion. I'm carrying a message from Marcus Satigenus, head of the cohort you requested as reinforcements."

"Deliver your message."

"By now the cohort must be two days away from here; yesterday at dawn, as we were marching across the valley where the so-called "salted" river meets the Garonne, we were stopped by the drivers of a coach coming from Lugdunum Convenarum and on its way to Tolosa."

"It was probably the one carrying Pomponius, Sennius and Lucius. Go on."

"Yes, it was their coach. They had probably stopped there for the night and had not yet resumed their journey."

"Please spare us the details. What happened?"

"All three of them are dead, Propraetor."

Rufus and Hadrianus were dumbfounded. Even Valerius, hearing it for the second time, felt the shock. In the void that seemed to have been created around them he felt like a man on the edge of a cliff about to fall into the abyss. Again he saw, only more clearly this time, what all this meant for the city. The three men had been murdered, that was obvious, and that would set off a chain of disasters: crying, sorrow and then, of course, hate and revenge. It was hard to predict how far this could go. He was like a player watching as each domino toppled the next and then the next and the next again while he was always too late to keep them from falling.

Hadrianus and Valerius both understood that after such a disaster nothing could halt the Propraetor's thirst for revenge: he would take the triple murder as a personal affront. The First Magistrate was shattered because the fate of the city had just been snatched out of his hands and he would meet the fate awaiting him at the very first misstep as governor of the civitas. The centurion thought that the harmony between Romans and Gauls that he had carefully worked to preserve was about to be shattered and that chaos might overwhelm the city.

After the messenger explained how the three young men had died, Rufus burst into such wild fury that no one knew how to react. He didn't feel sorry for the three young people and even less so for their parents; he was in a state close to madness, as if this triple murder had sent him back in time to a battle he had lost and had never forgotten. He no longer seemed aware of the words he was saying, he muttered incoherently about the Gauls, the young men, banishment; he was unable to control his body and was seized by fits that sent him rocking back and forth.

Valerius knew that kind of frantic despair. He had seen it on the battlefield; it was the kind of rage that seized the fighter as he was planting his dagger into the enemy's heart, expecting to feel only bitterness but then discovering his own reflection in the dead man's face. Killing the enemy didn't mean just taking his life; it also meant that the dying man was taking your image with him. That reflection had to be shattered or else it would drive you insane. Whatever you did you would never forget it.

After several minutes of frightening rage, Rufus stormed out and shut himself up in his room. Hadrianus and Valerius stood motionless unable to decide whether they should inform the parents of the three young men right away or wait for the cohort to bring back their bodies.

Valerius sent the messenger back to the fort so he could rest but warned him not to say a word about what was going on.

Hadrianus went to see if the Propraetor needed anything and was told that Rufus wanted to be left alone. After a few minutes, he reappeared: his voice was calm but he spoke like someone possessed. His face, his gestures, his entire body betrayed a cold unstoppable determination to see this affair through to the bloody end. Again and again using the same words, he repeated his one unshakable purpose: the Gauls must be crushed, the Barbarians must be destroyed, they must pay.

Valerius ventured to suggest that it was better not to take
any drastic action before they managed to shed some light on
the tragedy; Rufus though could barely be persuaded to wait
for the reinforcements before he launched a general offensive
against the Gallic neighborhood in the lower city.

Hadrianus felt that his world had come to an end. The
catastrophic turn of events effectively destroyed his plan and
trashed his agreement with Gedemo. There wasn't the slightest
chance anyone could dampen Rufus' thirst for war now. In an
instant he had become a puppet in the hands of a man intent
on destroying everything he had built up through the years: he
would have to dance the puppet master's dance and, in silent
impotence, watch the disaster unfold until it engulfed him. All
he could hope for from now on was that a few stones from the
edifice he had built would be left standing after he had gone.

XXII

Marcus Satigenus reached the fort two days later: Rufus didn't let the centurion's exhausted men get the rest they deserved, he immediately gave the order to arrest all the men in the families of the "long-haired" girls. He had decided to launch the operation that very same evening, just when the Gauls were having the last meal of the day: that was the time he could best surprise them at home. The number of men to be arrested was sixty two. The windows in the officers' barracks at the fort had to be sealed shut in order to turn the rooms into cells since the prison in the garrison was not large enough to hold all the prisoners. The Gauls had been crammed inside, eight to a room that would normally accommodate one visiting general or two legates. Valerius and Marcus were surprised that the Gauls offered no resistance when the legionaries burst into their homes but their faces betrayed their silent anger and the two centurions feared the worst in the days to come. They would have to watch the men in custody and try to prevent any uprising by the rest of the Gallic population. Valerius decided to tell his colleague what he thought of these methods:

"An army can be beaten, even by a smaller force, but an entire population can't be restrained even by a larger force."

"That may be, but a Propraetor is always right, even if he's the only one to think so, or when two centurions think he's wrong. Especially this Propraetor."

Even if Marcus Satigenus didn't himself entirely approve of Rufus's tactics, he disapproved even more of his colleague speaking his mind in such a brazen way. Valerius never brought up the subject again in his presence.

The entire Gallic neighborhood was quickly sealed off. Only five women, picked at random by Rufus, were allowed out: every day they crossed the line at a check point manned by legionaries, in order to bring food and water to the prisoners. As for the Gauls who worked for craftsmen or merchants in the Roman city, they also had to stay home until further notice and their employers had to do without them.

From that moment on it was as if Morpheus had put the city to sleep. The five young men's deaths were not viewed as random events but as the visible sign of the city's growing misfortune spreading like a disease. They were a presage of things to come while the gods punished the diseased and polluted city. In every household sacrifices were offered, animals were slaughtered and their entrails read for signs of the evils the gods might send and of who they might spare.

Only those who had lost their sons could claim to be suffering yet every Roman trembled with fear and locked himself up with his family in his home; death had spread its wings over the city like a black shroud and neither the troops posted around the Gallic neighborhood by Rufus nor the arrest of all the suspects could clear the air. Whatever it was that had caused the deaths of the three young men, the soldiers of the escort had been unable to prevent it: the killer had used magic or sorcery to defeat the soldiers' vigilance. No one could actually say what had killed the young Romans and many were convinced that it could not have been anything human. They had been poisoned, that much was established: their grimacing faces and blue tongues, their eyes rolled back and bloodshot all pointed to that explanation. The families' doctors had met and agreed that there could be no other explanation. But not one could to say which foods had been laced with poison. All the food found in the carriage, dishes that had been prepared by the family cooks and sweets that had been offered as gifts by their friends, had been fed to an entire pack of dogs and not a single one had fallen ill. Traces of opium had been found in an oriental pipe and the apothecary claimed that the poison had been mixed in with it, but that claim was impossible to corroborate. And where did the opium come from? The lack of any answers to these questions only comforted Rufus in his opinion that the murderer had to be a Gaul. To him there were no supernatural beings at work unless the Gauls themselves were to be considered sorcerers controlled by dark forces, something which he was prepared to believe.

The Bassei, the Melalae and the Sennicae would be allowed to bury their dead after the period of mourning and purification. There would be a single cortege, the mourners would walk through the Gallic neighborhood under escort and no Gaul would be allowed to attend. Sennius and Lucius would be buried, like their friends, by the side of the road under the walnut trees. Pomponius' remains were to be incinerated and his ashes carried to the family's villa in the Latium: Gallicus Melala had already announced that he intended to leave Lugdunum Convenarum and never return.

Pomponius' father was the empty shell of a man; he would much have preferred to die instead of his son and be spared the pain that tore him apart. He promised a reward for the arrest of the killer even though, as Rufus saw it, the killer had already been arrested. He was hiding among the imprisoned Convenes and it would take a few hours or at most a few days to force him out of the shadows, even if every man had to be tortured. The only thing that kept Gallicus alive was his desire for revenge. He would not rest until he could look into the murderer's eyes and watch him die; only then would he be able to shed some of the unbearable weight of his son's death. He would carry the urn to the Latium but let the killer bear the weight of his son's corpse into the netherworld! Until then, his offer of a reward would stand: twelve thousand silver denarii for him to feast his eyes on the killer, tied to a pole, in the forum.

He never spoke after that. No one saw him, his wife or their other children again. Like the Bassei and the Senicae, Gallicus' family shut itself up: their domus had become a temple filled with the lamentations of the mourners and the voices of the priests; torches burned day and night over the dead. The house smelled strongly of incense used to fight the smell of decomposing flesh and the odor of embalming plants that slowed the effect of the heat on the corpse

The stone cutter's men had started their work. Statitius Taurus had been instructed that, in deference to the families of Cracius and Balbius, the new tombs should not exceed the two preceding ones in size or decoration. The four identical mausoleums were not finished yet but they stood like a deathly guard of honor, identical, neatly aligned under the rows of trees at the entrance to the city.

The day before the ides of May had come to an end. Time had slowed and, for Rufus, the stage was set and Roman justice could be played out in the city for all to see: the families who mourned their dead, the imprisoned Convenes, the soldiers on guard at their posts, the frightened Romans and the Gauls confined to their neighborhood.

The beauty of the Pyrenees yielding to Spring, the budding flowers and scents, the warm caress of the sun's mild rays ... all that happy promise that usually swept up the inhabitants of the civitas and made them smile went completely unheeded. No one turned to nature to read her propitious omens, no one acknowledged the favors of the gods shining upon men in the colors and perfumes that she had donned to charm the humans' souls.

XXIII

Serenia, my sweet:

"My sweet", coming from me, it's as if a clumsy old bird of prey was trying to clutch a tender twig in its embrace. And yet what I need right now, and what is fast escaping me never to return, is sweetness, gentleness. There is nothing that can give me a moment's rest in the ceaseless flow of events. Oh, if only time could stop and give me just a few instants of eternity before plunging headlong into the succession of days and months! My thoughts are locked inside me and when I put them into words for you, they flow in my throat like a soothing balm and spill unto the desk where I write. The page is like a wound, my fingers are spreading a healing balm and my pain is soothed for a while. In those moments, you are my sweet, my tender Serenia.

And yet, inside me, the words hurt: they keep saying that the murderer is not a Gaul.

The words I've just written make me tremble. I'm afraid. When I write these words I write against Rufus and setting things down on paper against Rufus means that I'm writing against Rome's justice.

Against Rome.

I must be mad.

Or else, Rome is mad.

The killer is not a Gaul. I'm sure of it. I know it. It's more than an intuition, or even a conviction, it's the truth. The first murder threw me off the scent like everyone else: the Gallic dagger seemed to imply hand to hand combat or maybe a surprise attack...I thought it must be a Gaul. I never questioned the idea. But then came Balbius' murder and the method didn't fit. A Convene would never have used a snake to kill an enemy. Who among them could have purchased a North African Rhinoceros viper without raising some eyebrows? It was impossible.

Then the murder of the three remaining boys convinced me that I was right. Lucius, Sennius and Pomponius were under such tight guard that it would have been impossible for a Gaul to come near them. How could one of them have hidden poison in their carriage? I tried talking to Rufus. But he wouldn't even allow me to explain my theory. For him the murderer can only be a Convene; anything else is unthinkable. I insisted but Rufus Riego is a Propraetor and I'm just a centurion. When he says I'm wrong, then I'm wrong. I have to keep quiet.

I think he's mad.

I shudder but not because I'm afraid. Because it's horrible. He's arrested sixty two Convenes and among them their leader Gedemo, the city's Fourth Magistrate. He's declared war on the Gauls. The killer is not among them. The city is divided in two camps. What will he do now?

The Gauls are strong and proud, vanquished but not crushed and still rebellious. How will it all end?

My sword and my shield are in the service of this man.

I tremble at the horror of it.

XXIV

The prisoners were lined up in eight rows. They were counted as they stepped out of their cells and then counted again when they were made to form a square in the courtyard of the fort. Two centuries of soldiers surrounded the Convenes, spears at the ready, prepared to plunge them into the tight mass of bodies at the first sign of resistance and a dozen archers were posted on the palisade as a precaution. It was very unlikely that the Gallic population inside the security perimeter could manage to breach the line of legionaries, but Rufus had decided to take the kind of measures a general would take in the event a city was attacked by barbarian hordes.

Rufus had watched the prisoners being moved from their cells and lined up by the decurions. He went nowhere without his personal guard from Tolosa. Apart from them, only Valerius Musa and Marcus Satigenus had been allowed to stand by his side and make sure everything went smoothly, even though they didn't yet know what the Propraetor had in mind. He had told them only that he was going to talk to the prisoners, that he wanted them in rows the courtyard but facing the sun. The legionaries maneuvered at a run and barked out their orders. But the Gauls kept a proud, ominous silence throughout. Gedemo, who remained their unquestioned leader, gave the example: he refused to run but did not do anything to provoke the soldiers. The irons on his legs, the two nights he had spent in the uncomfortable cell did not make him hold his head any lower: he looked straight ahead and stood in an almost warlike attitude that impressed Valerius. The centurion admired the chief's proud bearing and took it to be the sign of a great determination. Rufus' task was not going to be easy. The Propraetor was now striding back and forth at the head of the assembled prisoners with his hands behind his back, like a general reviewing his troops. He looked down at the ground, waiting for the right time to speak. He hadn't even glanced at Gedemo.

More orders were shouted, the last remaining prisoners aligned, then, little by little, there was silence. Rufus was waiting.

The Convenes stood as straight as their leg irons allowed them to, showing Rufus that two days' imprisonment had not cowed them.

Finally, complete silence was established; for a few seconds, the only things still stirring were the men's shadows projected by the sun on the ground of the courtyard. There wasn't the slightest sound from the stables, not even a bird flittered across the courtyard, the uniforms' leather straps didn't creak... Everyone waited for Rufus to speak. He chose the moment when all were holding their breath to shout:

"Convenes! Yours is a proud and brave people; Rome recognized that and did not enslave you. You are nevertheless a defeated people: either you blend into the empire or you disappear. You are my prisoners but your honor has not been impugned. That is not what I wish to do, on the contrary. I wish to give you your honor back by cleansing your ranks of the man whose actions has sullied your people. Ever since Augustus defeated you, you have had to live by Rome's justice. Five Romans dishonored your daughters; Cracius Vespasianus and Balbius Iassus payed with their lives. I rendered judgment on the others. Pomponius Melala, Lucius Senica and Sennius Basseus were sentenced to exile; they had accepted their sentence but one of you decided that it was not enough and took their lives. All three of them were found dead from poisoning, in the carriage that was carrying them to Tolosa.

The prisoners looked at each other: So the rumor was true!

Rufus paid no attention and went on:

"Rome cannot allow a criminal to take justice into his own hands. Whoever committed these crimes must pay and if you try to protect him by keeping quiet all of you will pay.

Rufus' voice echoed against the palisade. The Propraetor paused and tried to measure the effect his words were having on the Convenes, but their faces didn't betray any feelings. All were again completely still. Rufus decided to strike harder:

"Five Romans have died, five young men. Five Convenes of the same age will die tomorrow morning. After that, a Convene will be executed every day at sunrise until you hand over the murderer."

A ripple went through the prisoners' ranks. Rufus was satisfied that his words had the effect he had hoped for. Still, Gedemo's face was a blank. So the Propraetor came up to him, stood with his legs slightly apart and stared him in the face as if he were challenging him to a duel; four legionaries stood at his side to keep Gedemo from lunging at him. He pointed to Bellovese, Gedemo's eldest son and like a Caesar at the games, turned his thumb down:

"You."

Gedemo glanced at his son.

"And you."

Rufus was pointing to Gedemo's second son, Lutarios. This time, Gedemo stepped forward but the raised spears kept him back.

"You and you and you also."

Rufus had designated Dorix, who was to marry Gedemo's daughter and thus would become part of his family, Vallorix, his youngest, and Brennos, one of Gedemo's nephews.

The old Gallic chief was shaken, he breathed hard and his jaws tightened to suppress a cry. Rufus saw it and he felt an intense joy. He relished the sight of the man's impotent rage: it confirmed that even the greatest goodwill could not survive an attack on what was most precious to a father, were he the strongest of men.

Gedemo wasn't the only one hit hard. Valerius Musa also could hardly contain himself. Rufus had not told him about his plans and now they had been unveiled in all their horror for all to see, Romans and Convenes. The injustice of it made his blood boil. Such an arbitrary, ignoble use of power could only be the mark of a sick mind. Had Rufus thought about the consequences? There would be no reprieve after this. Valerius tried to get Marcus Satigenus' attention but the centurion stared straight ahead with an empty look on his face. Was it possible he agreed with all this?

"As I said, tomorrow morning you will be hanged in the forum."

The five men Rufus had condemned pulled on their chains to solicit support from their companions. Lutarios stepped forward but, instantly, one of Rufus' personal guards struck him in the stomach: he doubled up and fell on his knees, gasping for air. At that moment, the ranks of the prisoners moved almost imperceptibly and the experienced legionaries reacted immediately by raising their spears. The Convenes did not move.

The Propraetor's entire body seemed flushed with pleasure: he smiled as he heard the thud of the legionaries elbow against the young Convene's flesh; he relished the sound of Lutarios' strangled moan.

Valerius had seen this kind of violence before and had hoped he would not have to witness it again. The cruel grin on Rufus' face brought back scenes of unbridled violence after the battle: prisoners being beaten and trampled to death, women being raped. But it was at a different time and in a different place: it was during the war with the months of exhaustion, privations and waiting that had to be relieved; more than that, fear had to be exorcised; the enemy had to be humiliated so that one could heal, the myth of his prowess had to be destroyed and the enemy reduced to ordinary mortals. Valerius thought he was done with such horrors. But Propraetor Rufus Riego brought barbarity back to this corner of Aquitania. Why? Hadn't this land become his home, hadn't he been living here for many years?

What was it that fueled such hatred in the man?

Valerius turned again to look at his colleague but Marcus continued to ignore the question burning in his eyes. Having been posted in Tolosa for many years he knew that no one ever contradicted Rufus Riego. He knew it from experience. It wasn't only Rufus' reputation that kept him from saying anything; he had seen the Propraetor's anger with his own eyes. When it erupted the last thing to do was to try to reason him or oppose him; the best thing to do was to turn away. Even the Proconsul in Tolosa did not risk it: Rufus had friends in the highest places in Rome and he was free to act as recklessly as he wished and never have to account for anything. The Proconsul was appointed by the Senate but the Propraetor represented Rome's justice in the provinces and, since Augustus' ascent, his power was greater than the Proconsul's. The emperor himself had named him to this post and he had become

Augustus' eyes and ears and his spokesman in the region around Tolosa: Rufus Riego feared no one and everyone behaved as if *he* were the emperor.

He would let Valerius figure it out by himself. Certainly, he should be more careful; he should not try to protect the Gauls because Rufus was their sworn enemy ever since his six year old son had been murdered by the Volsques. The tribesmen had kidnapped the boy along with two other children, the Proconsul's son among them, on the road from Rome and they had offered to exchange them against three of their own men imprisoned in Tolosa. It had happened eighteen years before, during an uprising of the Gauls in the same region of the province. At the time, Rufus Riego was a young judge recently appointed to assist the new Proconsul of Tolosa. The Proconsul had refused to free the three Volsques and the tribe had the children and their nurses beheaded. In retaliation Caesar ordered that the tribe be hunted down and every man, woman and child killed. Still, ever since then, Rufus was consumed with hatred for all Gauls. The flame inside him burned steadily: no amount of blood could ever extinguish it.

But why reveal all this to Valerius Musa? Why should he help a centurion who seemed to have lost all sense of hierarchy and of his place in the order of things, which was all the way at the bottom. He had been living in this peaceful corner of the empire for too long. Marcus had been shocked by what he had seen in the fort: it looked more like a thermal resort for vacationing Romans than a military outpost. And now even decurions thought they could disapprove of the orders they received. Hard to believe.

What did Valerius think he was going to achieve? Did he expect Rufus to listen to him and turn into a magnanimous, well-intentioned friend of the Gauls, just because a centurion had shown him that, in all conscience, treating them as he did was not reasonable, and not humane? Marcus felt he would enjoy seeing Rufus put the centurion in his place if he ever dared oppose him.

But Valerius said nothing.

Rufus turned away and, without a word, flicking his wrist over his shoulder in a gesture of contempt, waved the prisoners away: they were to be led back to their cells. The Convenes were still standing in a perfect square. All of a sudden, before any had moved, a voice rang out like an arrow striking its target. Gedemo shouted:

"Roman!"

Immediately, the legionaries made a circle of their weapons around the Propraetor: nothing could harm him, not even the Gaul's words. But Gedemo wasn't threatening, he had not moved. Rufus held his hand up to stop his men. He smiled the smile of a man who has managed to subdue a wild beast. He finally had him, that old wolf, who had proudly resisted every attempt to tame him. He was surprised: it had taken so little time to break him. It was almost disappointing.

"I'm the one you are looking for. I killed Cracius, Balbius and the others. Let my people go free, they played no part in this. Let them go home."

Rufus stood there, looking at Gedemo. He was thinking: in the Gaul's situation, what would he have done? Exactly what Gedemo was attempting now, he would try to save his sons' lives.

Just for an instant, he thought of his own son and was again filled with hatred; or rather his hatred was rekindled since it never died. It lived inside him. It kept him alive.

What would he do in Gedemo's place? He would confess to the crimes in order to create the greatest possible commotion: a Gallic chief involved in such heinous crimes! It would resonate all the way back to Rome. The sheer magnitude of the event would make Rufus forget the five dead young men and the five Convenes he had just condemned to death. But there was no stopping the Propraetor's justice; it would strike as surely as the sword, as inevitably as fate decreed by the gods.

"By denouncing yourself you may have saved the lives of the men who were to be put to death every day but you will not spare the others the price I have decided they should pay for the five lives you have taken. I said there would be five young Convenes taken for the five young Romans."

Gedemo threw himself headlong against the Propraetor in an attempt to ram into his belly but he was immediately struck by the legionaries just as his son had been. He fell to the ground. The dust from the dry dirt of the courtyard mingled with the sweat on his face.

"You're nothing but a stinking rat, a coward. My people will avenge us. You will not leave Lugdunum Convenarum alive."

"We all die some day, that's true. But I know when you and your sons are going to die: it will be tomorrow. You will have no descendants because the only child you have left is your daughter, the slut, and you banished her. That, as a matter of fact, is the only honorable thing I'm prepared to grant you did. As for the day of my death, I don't think my days are destined to end here, at least not yet. Your threats may make you feel better but they have no effect on me because your people, the Convenes, no longer exist: you all belong to Rome and you should finally accept the fact that you have lost the war."

With these words Rufus turned back to the legionaries and drawing up a half circle with his arm signaled that the prisoners should all be driven into the barracks and the courtyard cleared of them. Valerius watched them go in one by one, dumbstruck. Canius and Flaccus approached wanting to know what the explanation was for all this but Valerius had none. It was all wrong. He didn't believe Gedemo was guilty despite his having confessed.

"He wanted to save his sons, that's all."

"Or he wanted to die with them since he knew they were doomed", ventured Flaccus: he also could not believe Gedemo was the man they were looking for. They had often seen this during their campaigns: no one was more ferocious than a father whose son was dead because he had nothing left to lose. Such a man was willing to die in order to kill.

Valerius' thoughts went back to the Latium and to his two sons: would he also have died rather than let Gnaeus and Publius be killed? He wasn't so sure anymore. He couldn't answer the question and it made him feel bad.

He decided to go against the rules set up by Rufus who had forbidden any contact with the prisoners. He waited for the Propraetor to leave, tried to avoid being seen by Marcus whose distrust was palpable and walked into the barracks. The legionaries on duty hesitated at first to let him through but figured that since he was the centurion commanding the garrison he probably knew what he was doing. Without wasting any time, Valerius went to Gedemo's cell.

"Gedemo. Gedemo!"

The old chief got up and came to the wood panel that had been hastily fitted on the door in each barrack to keep the prisoners inside.

"Is that you Valerius?"

"Yes, it's me."

"What do you want?"

"I know you didn't kill Cracius and his friends. I can still try and save you but you must tell me everything you know."

"All I can say is that the murderer is not among my people. No one among the prisoners is guilty of these crimes."

"How can you be so certain?"

"Hadrianus had warned me that we were all going to be arrested and I called a meeting of all the families three days ago. Had the killer been among us, I would have found it out then. It's a question of honor. No Convene would have put all of his people at risk; it's against our code of conduct."

"So who is it?"

"I don't know."

"Why did you confess then?"

"What are you doing here centurion Valerius?"

Valerius had been leaning his head against the panel; he stood back like a thief caught in the act. Marcus was slowly coming toward him in the corridor.

"I was talking to Gedemo for my investigation."

"There is no investigation. Gedemo confessed to his crimes, you have no business here."

"Marcus, listen. I've been posted here for eight years. I know Gedemo personally. He is not the murderer: Rufus is making a terrible mistake."

"You're the one who's making a mistake, Valerius: you are disobeying orders by talking to someone who has been condemned to death. The truth is you have been living here too long. But I can fix that if you continue to thwart justice."

"Forget your rank and the hierarchy for once, Marcus and think for yourself: consider the consequences; what's at stake here is the stability of the empire in this part of the province."

"That's exactly what I mean: I will not forget my rank and neither should you. What would become of Rome if centurions suddenly got it into their heads that they should "think"? Go back to your quarters or I'll arrest you and put you in jail with your Gallic friends."

Valerius gave up: Marcus refused to understand; but as he passed his colleague he couldn't keep from muttering between his teeth: "Dumb as a doornail."

"What did you say?"

"Nothing, Marcus. Go on obeying orders. That's the only thing you know how to do."

He walked down the corridor without turning back. Had
he looked back though, he would have seen the rage on
Marcus' face and his clenched fists.

XXV

Lorus had just finished reading out the merchants' list of grievances but it was obvious Hadrianus and Caius Retus weren't listening. It was to be expected of course that the city's affairs would be somewhat neglected, considering what had happened in the past few weeks, but ever since Gedemo and his men had been locked up in the fort, things had deteriorated even more. It was now impossible for the Gauls to go about their business freely and the blockade of the lower city that Rufus had set up hurt business considerably. The Roman businessmen complained and took it out on Lorus. He was unsure as to who was really in charge within the civitas and so he found it increasingly difficult to play his customary role of go-between. He couldn't help thinking that he was the only one to still care about the city, now that the Quattuorvirate had been reduced to a duumvirate composed of Caius Retus and Hadrianus.

As the oldest, Caius was dean of the council, but he had never played a major role. He must be deeply disturbed by the happenings, all the murders, and Gedemo's arrest: he was incapable of making any decision.

Hadrianus was more wrapped up in his own problems that in those of the merchants and craftsmen's guilds. The Propraetor held him responsible for the city's present situation since, in his view, he had failed. He thought back with bitter irony to his plans for a trophy in honor of Augustus; he had thought it would allow him to get back in favor with the emperor. Things were looking up; he had started believing in the future and then, just as he thought he had found the way to regaining his status, the gods had chosen to strike: they had sent him this terrible calamity. Everything he had accomplished, all the years of penance for his former opposition and, after the fall of the Republic, his exile from Rome, his new life here where he had started from scratch, all his efforts to build a Roman civitas, to demonstrate his goodwill and to erase the past... all that had been destroyed in the space of a few weeks.

When Lorus entered his master's house he found it unusually quiet. There wasn't a sound from the boys' room whereas their noisy games used to interrupt their father's work; the slaves went about their chores in silence. Everything seemed to have come to a standstill; even the harp Lorus was used to hearing whenever he came was silent. Every member of the household could sense the seriousness of the situation and kept quiet as if to support their master in his deliberations.

He scratched his throat and succeeded in catching Hadrianus' attention.

"Ah? Yes. Thank you Lorus."

"What should I say to the merchants, master?"

"Tell them to ... well, I don't know. Tell them I can't say anything for the moment. Tell them to talk to Rufus Riego. I'm not the one making decisions for now and I'm not sure how long this situation will continue."

Lorus had known Hadrianus for many years and was only too aware that his master could become totally obsessed with whatever was troubling him. What was bad for Hadrianus might actually be good for Lorus: if power at the top was weakened, he stood to gain. After Gedemo was arrested and

Calidius Iassus had announced he was leaving, the Quattuorvirate had lost two of its members and Lorus saw his role increasing proportionately. Now, Hadrianus, by refusing to talk to the merchants was giving his manager a free rein: in the eyes of the population, he would become the key person in the management of the city's business. He knew that the guilds were the opinion makers. Being closer to them, he understood this fact perfectly whereas Hadrianus, the "honestior", the nobleman, remained characteristically aloof.

Caius Retus poured himself a cup of wine and offered some to Hadrianus, who declined.

"You are blameless, Hadrianus. That Propraetor has managed to rekindle a long extinguished fire. His brutal methods will do no good. We will complain to the Proconsul as soon as this is over."

Hadrianus looked at the Second Magistrate as if he were seeing him for the first time; he suddenly realized how old the man was. "He looks like a senile old man", he thought to himself. His old friend was completely out of his league. He had not the faintest idea of what was at stake. "When all this is over", he had said. That was almost laughable. Hadrianus leaned back against the red wool pillows and breathed out slowly. For a while, all one could hear was Hadrianus sighing, and the squeaking of one of the legs of the couch and just then, as Lorus was wondering whether he should stay or leave, there was a sharp knock on the front door. Hadrianus knew it had to be Valerius: he had this way of letting the knocker fall hard against the panel.

A few moments later, the ostiarius appeared at the door.

"The centurion Valerius is asking to see you, master."

"What is it now? Let him in." A few more seconds went by and Valerius arrived. He looked stricken.

"Salve, Hadrianus. Salve Caius, Lorus."

"What is it? You look as though you've seen a ghost."

"I'm glad to find all three of you here. It's about Rufus Riego."

"What about Rufus? What else has he done?"

"He's just decreed that five young Convenes would be executed tomorrow morning, among them Gedemo's three sons and Dorix and Brennos, the sons of Gedemo's brother."

"What!"

Hadrianus sat up so suddenly that the whole couch creaked under his weight; this time though, his voice boomed, covering any other sound. A deep red hue spread over his cheeks, his forehead, his eyes even. Caius was trying to understand:

"But why?"

"As a reprisal for each death: one Convene shall die for each dead Roman."

"He's lost his mind, Gedemo is going to order his people to rise up against us: it's obvious."

Hadrianus again let out a cry at the unthinkable madness. He was no longer thinking of his position as First Magistrate or the way he would be seen in Tolosa, but of the cataclysm Rufus was about to unleash. He couldn't let this mad government official, blinded by his own desire for revenge, continue to destroy everything he had built up, in the vain hope of putting his private demons to rest. Hadrianus knew what had happened to Rufus' son but this was going too far: he would put a stop to it.

Valerius added:

"Gedemo has confessed to the five murders, but he's not saying the truth: it is obvious he did it in order to save his sons, and also because Rufus had threatened to have a prisoner executed every day until the murderer was found. Gedemo knew the killer was not among his people, so he confessed to protect them."

"How does he know none of his people are guilty?"

"Because the killer is not a Gaul."

If someone had told Hadrianus his house in the Latium had collapsed he wouldn't have been more shattered. He was dumbstruck.

"I'm convinced of it myself now. Also, the murderer is not a man, but a woman."

At that point, Hadrianus' repeated cries ended up alarming the entire household. A few slaves came running to the office to see if their master was alright. Staia came running in as well followed by Claudia: she had probably been dressing and all she was wearing was a light tunic folded over her shoulders. The boys ran in from the kitchen, their lips sticky from the honey and poppy cakes that the cook prepared once a month. They all pushed aside the entrance curtain and stood hoping that Valerius or Hadrianus would explain.

But Hadrianus waved them away, grumbled something and sat back against the pillows. Still, while the family scrambled off to avoid provoking another outburst, Staia stayed behind and looked fixedly at her father. Her face showed no fear and he thought there was something else, that she wanted to tell him something. It was only a fleeting impression but again, he thought that his daughter was truly extraordinary; maybe she was the only one who truly understood him or, maybe, on the contrary, she was the one he understood the least. The thought brought on a wave of melancholy. He didn't know where it came from or why he felt it but, in the end, it made him look down to avoid Staia's eyes. His daughter noticed it and turned away to follow her mother and brothers out of the room.

This time Hadrianus almost whispered his questions to Valerius.

"Are you suggesting the murderer is a Roman woman? Do you realize what you're saying?"

"I'm not suggesting anything, the evidence speaks for itself. What does a father whose daughter has been dishonored do? He draws his sword and fights. What father, what brother would slip a snake into the bed of the man who has attacked his daughter or his sister? That is the mark of someone for whom physical combat is not an option. The same thing can be said of murder by poison: these methods imply the same absence of physical contact with the victims, the same reliance on a measure of chance; after all, someone else, an innocent person, could have ingested the poison or not all three of the intended victims could have been killed, one could have escaped. I see the hand of a woman in this."

"And why not a Convene woman?"

"The poisonous snake from Africa. Think about it: it takes money to pay a shady dealer to have it shipped discreetly. And what about the poison? No trace of it was ever found. That requires a great deal of sophisticated planning; it's not the work of a Gaul blinded by anger. Not the way a Gaul would strike. There's also the fact that the three young men were kept under constant guard and that the poison had to have been placed in their carriage before they left by someone who had permission to go near it or to visit them. I questioned the legionaries who guarded the young men that day from the moment they left the curia. They had no contact whatsoever with the Gauls. On the other hand, I was able to establish the list of all the Romans they saw before they left."

Valerius handed the magistrate a list and Hadrianus immediately felt a pang of anguish; it struck him with such force, he knew exactly where it came from: this was the mirror image of what had taken place before. He saw himself in Gedemo's place in the curia a few days before, looking at the list, fearful that his own daughter's name might be on it. He remembered Claudia and Staia returning from their visits to the Melalae, the Bassei and the Senicae the night before the men's departure. They had had sweets prepared for the journey and they had been to each house to say goodbye and wish the young men a pleasant journey. Hadrianus turned pale; he felt that everyone in the room, Valerius, Caius, Lorus, were reading his thoughts; they had seen his reaction, they knew. They didn't speak but Hadrianus heard their voices shouting their accusations: she's the one; Staia, your daughter Staia is the killer; she's the one who killed Cracius, the man she was going to marry and who betrayed her; you saw the way she looked at you just now. Your daughter was always strange, she's not like the others. She's the one. You're the father of a killer.

Valerius saw how Hadrianus had reacted. He realized all of a sudden that not only did Staia's and Claudia's names figure on the list but that among all the people who had visited the three exiles , none had better reason than Staia to feel offended by Cracius. That would explain why the first one to be killed had been her fiancé and why that crime had been the most violent; it was a crime of passion. How could he not have thought of it before? And now, fool that he was, he had presented his findings to Hadrianus, the father of the probable killer.

Hadrianus had regained his composure; his mind started to work again and with it his will to fight for his daughter. He knew that the ghastly insight had also struck Valerius.

Both men looked at each other: they realized that from now on they were on opposite sides. Something even more terrifying entered Hadrianus' mind: his own daughter's life now depended on what happened to his colleague Gedemo. He could still try to save the five innocent young men but Gedemo had to die so that his daughter could be saved; if Valerius could prove her guilt, he would go down with her. He went on pretending to be angry and dismayed but he had decided to keep Rufus in the dark: he must let him think that he had found the real murderer. Valerius' goal was the exact opposite: it was, and always had been, to find the real culprit and clear the Gauls whose execution could plunge the city into a bloodbath. But he had no illusions: he did not stand a chance against Hadrianus Trevius, senator and first magistrate of the civitas. Whatever hopes he might still have harbored, they were destroyed when the magistrate spoke:

"It will be difficult to convince Rufus to go back on his decision. A Gaul had been convicted, just as he wished from the beginning and he also freely confessed to his crime... I don't see how you could unmask this woman murderer before tomorrow morning."

Hadrianus was right, and Valerius knew it. From the beginning, he had been unable to convince Rufus to search for the murderer among the Romans, so how could he hope to do so now that Gedemo had come forward and confessed? He was only a centurion and without Rufus' authorization he could not take the theory he had just outlined to the two magistrates any further, especially since the First Magistrate himself had every reason to not support it. Valerius, after all, had no solid proof. Hadrianus had nothing to fear from Valerius Musa; the glint of irony in the magistrate's eyes didn't escape him. Caius closed the case by making an appeal to caution:

"We had better not get involved in any of this. Let Rufus Riego take responsibility for his actions. When the Proconsul learns that he started a riot and that it led to bloodshed, he won't hesitate to punish the Propraetor for his violent methods. We will then have every opportunity to argue that we never approved of him."

Valerius said nothing and there was silence in the house. Once again, he was struck by the unusual atmosphere. But he gave up and said:

"You're right. Nothing we can do will save Gedemo but we can still save the five young Convenes. They are clearly innocent: even Rufus doesn't doubt it. Having them executed is an arbitrary and unjust act and the Convenes won't accept it: it will give them a reason to rise up against us. They can probably accept that Gedemo be put to death because he confessed but if we put his three sons to death and his nephew Brennos, and young Dorix… that will really look like gangland justice."

"What do you propose to do?"

"We must ask for an audience with Rufus, all three of us, and attempt to convince him, one last time."

"That won't do any good", said Caius.

He didn't feel like risking the wrath of the Propraetor. Valerius didn't confront Hadrianus, rather, he begged him with his eyes: they expressed as clearly and as firmly as he could make them that he agreed to let Gedemo die, that Staia would be spared, but that he must help him save the five young men and put a stop to the bloodletting. There had to be a truce between the two of them. Could Hadrianus afford to agree to it?

"As soon as he comes home tonight, I'll ask him for an audience. But, until then, please leave me alone. I have things to do."

Caius Retus and Lorus took their leave. Valerius followed behind them, but after they had gone, he stopped and looked at Hadrianus. He did not move, nor did he say anything, he expected no words of justification, he just wanted to stand in the same room with the abject man who was going to keep quiet in order to save his daughter, and breathe the same air. Again he asked himself the question he had asked when he saw Gedemo readily giving up his life to save others: in Hadrianus' place would he too let an innocent man die in order to save his daughter's life? Once again, he found he had no answer. Would he choose to save one of his sons? Would he refuse? He wasn't sure. Would he be a good father and show the right example? Would he be a bad father if he sacrificed his own flesh and blood in the name of an ideal of justice?

He turned around and left the room.

XXVI

"Why Staia? Why did you do it?"

Hadrianus was bent over his daughter; she was leaning against him. They were face to face, forehead against forehead. She did not cry. He did.

I had never seen him cry. I thought men never cried.

Are they all like him, or is my father different?

She would never find the answer to these questions, she had decided she would never let one of those beings touch her. Never. She would rather die. Or kill.

"Why, Staia?"

He smells bad. He has bad breath. Do men all smell bad?

She would never know.

"Say something, please, I beg you."

Why, always why. Is it so difficult to understand? When a dog bites, it's put down. When a tree threatens to fall on a house, it's cut down.

"Is it because he was unfaithful? Is that it? I can understand, Staia. You are my daughter: I can understand your anger when you found out where Cracius had been that night."

That night? What about all the other nights? How many other nights, before that one?

"But why kill Balbius? Why Pomponius and Sennius… why Lucius? You grew up with him. They never hurt you."

They didn't. "We didn't do anything, nothing bad, we were bored. We just wanted to have some fun"…

Fun: they took advantage of those poor naïve girls, violated them, robbed them of something they had nurtured for years to offer it to the man of their life, and branded them forever. Worse than rape, it was a lie: they made them agree to the rape, they made them want it with all their heart. A woman who has been raped can hate the man who despoiled her, but a woman who has been tricked has only herself to blame, her own credulity.

They collected girls like prizes in a game that promised a trophy at the end. And we, their future wives, were supposed to wait for them patiently and admire their virility, wait for the day we would be theirs so they could mount us and remember the other women they had.

For them, we are all just mares to be mounted, objects to be owned, objects that provide power over other men.

In the end, it's all a man's game. I stole a part in a man's play: that's the crime I committed.

Cracius and the other men never really lusted over these girls: they used them to prove themselves, to measure themselves against one another. Women are nothing but a stepping stone: we help men get on a higher horse, a prouder, more beautiful beast.

"Please answer me; I can understand, but you have to explain."

You can understand? I'm not so sure, dear father! Can you understand what we have to endure, we girls, before we can become women; can you know all the things we must leave behind in order to become a wife?

"Staia, I'm your father. I have the right to know."

Men: what do men leave behind? What do they have to lose? You're my father, yes you are. I think you have been a good father or at least a loving father. But first and foremost, you are a man. You cannot understand and you don't have the right to understand.

"You don't seem to realize what this means. You could spend your life in prison for this."

Prison, life in a cell? So what? Is life spent grooming myself, painting my face and adorning myself for someone like Cracius any better? Emptiness and vanity: I'd rather have prison.

"You know your mother and I will never abandon you. We are with you, we will save you but you've got to talk to me."

You and mother. You make me laugh, father. Look at yourselves! You, constantly poring over your ledgers, your deals and your accounts, constantly ruminating about your past glory and your uncertain future, amassing a fortune in the hope of returning to Rome in style; and mother, forced to find some kind of satisfaction in her endlessly changing wardrobe, her only contact with you being when you discuss the guest list for the next banquet, and of course the list is always, forever, the same one because Lugdunum Convenarum isn't big enough to contain two different lists of guests.

"You must swear to me that this madness is over. It's turned out very badly, you know. Rufus Riego is convinced the murderer is a Gaul and he's preparing to unleash another war between the Convenes and the Romans."

I have never seen anyone more abject than Rufus Riego.

"He is going to put five Convenes to death tomorrow at dawn, young people, people your age."

Staia pulled away violently and sat up. There were still no tears on her face but only an expression of utter horror. Father and daughter looked at each other for a long time, with tenderness and cruelty, love and regret. Hadrianus understood then that she would not tell him anything, that she would fight him with silence, all her life, and that she would never speak to him again. In spite of love, and the past, there could be no future. He accepted it, but he went on:

"Gedemo will be executed tomorrow."

Gedemo...Epotsorovida... Cracius.

"He gave himself up to save his family but his three sons will die with him tomorrow morning. They are those to be executed."

I didn't want that. The gods are my witness, I never wanted that.

"Rufus is mad: there is nothing we can do to save them now. But you must promise me you will stop, otherwise you will be suspected. Valerius Musa has already figured out it was you but you mustn't fear: he can't prove anything."

Fear? What should I fear when these men are going to die because of me? They didn't do anything, it's not the same thing. Gedemo. His three sons … and the others, all the Convenes, all innocent men. Even in death, Cracius, Balbius, Pomponius, Lucius and Sennius continue to insult their people. I killed five men: I never hesitated, I did it almost with my own hands, but now, innocent men are going to die because of me! No, that can't be! I can't let that happen!

"Staia!"

Hadrianus had lost patience: he shouted.

"Talk to me. At least give me a sign that you agree, that you will stop this. All the men who did those things to the girls, the whole group, you…. They're all dead. Promise me it's over, otherwise I will have to have you locked up. By Vesta I will, even if you are my daughter and even though I love you."

Staia gave in: She nodded, pushed her father away and lay down on her bed with her back turned to him. She started crying silently; Hadrianus saw her shoulders heave with silent sobs.

He was dumbfounded as he always was whenever he tried to see into his daughter's heart. She had always been so difficult to understand, so different from the other girls her age.

Her mother said she was reserved.

Others said mysterious.

She was passionate.

She was unyielding.

She frightened him.

XXVII

Serenia my love:
How long will I have to bear this? How long will I be able to bear it? I take the horse out every day now, sometimes even twice a day. I go back to the peak, under the oak tree and I look at the Pyrenees with the setting sun in my back. Have I told you about this spot? It's high up and from there I feel as if I could look over the horizon and see you, even though it's impossible. I sit in the tall grass and I bury myself in it and I hide. I hide from all the horrors around me and I try to keep them from clinging to me.

The empire wields justice only to consolidate its power: it doesn't care who is punished so long as the blow, when it strikes, is louder than the people's discontent.

My role in all of this sickens me. Have I served Rome for twenty years for this?

Every day it gets harder for me to stop at the peak and not ride on to another peak and then another ... farther and farther until it's easier to go away than to go back.

There's no one to confide in. Not even you: would you understand it if you saw how I try to hold onto each day so night won't come and with it another day, because the new day will be worse than the one before? As time goes by, the burden gets heavier and I have a growing feeling I don't belong here. All the decurions can say when I complain is "That's the way things are, there's nothing you can do. Nothing." They prefer to hide behind high walls: not the kind of wall that protects you from an outside attack, but the kind of wall that keeps you safe from yourself, from doubts, from the truth out there. What they fear the most is that they might slip beyond the wall with me.

So now I keep falling down, fast, because there's no one to stop me.

Serenia, if only you were here! Maybe you would smile while you listened and you would stroke my head free of the bits of straw from the wheat fields near the via Appia where we used to lie; maybe you would come with me to this peak to watch the setting sun, or would you also stay inside the walls with all those who don't want to know and who probably think I'm mad?

I love you, Serenia.

I don't remember ever having said that to you. Maybe I'm not writing these words to you: maybe Serenia vanished a long time ago into the labyrinth of my mind, where solitude is erasing the past bit by bit.

I don't know, but I know it makes me feel better to hear myself say I love you.

And I watch the yellow flowers swaying in the breeze. Tomorrow, there will be bodies swaying from the scaffold.

XXVIII

The setting chosen for the execution was worthy of the games in the Circus Maximus in Rome. The carpenters requisitioned by Rufus had only a few hours to set everything up, but they had finished their work by the time the centurion's men marched slowly into the forum with the chained prisoners: there was a platform for the dignitaries of the civitas, among them the members of the council and their families, and, of course, the gallows for six men which had been raised high enough so that the crowd, even in the farthest corner of the forum, could see them. Rufus expected a large crowd and wanted everyone to be able to enjoy the spectacle.

All the garrison's men were on duty to prevent any commotion from the crowd. The platform had been built almost on the exact spot where Hadrianus and Lorus had planned to erect the trophy to honor Augustus; it faced the gallows ten steps away, and beyond them, the fortress with its wall lit up by the rising sun.

Hadrianus, Caius Retus, Lorus and Valerius Musa were all there, sitting on either side of Rufus Riego, in the first row. Behind them sat the victims' families, silent and dignified, waiting for the moment when Gedemo's body would hang above the ground and hoping it would make their grief more bearable. Gedemo's death was the natural outcome of what had happened but they didn't feel that the five young Convenes' death was right: they knew it would only serve to re-kindle their pain. They were the same age and would share the same fate as their own sons.

Valerius and Hadrianus had failed to convince Rufus to spare them; their execution would almost surely provoke the anger of the Gauls and unleash a rebellion. But it became clear to them that, far from being worried at the prospect of a rebellion, Rufus was hoping for one in order to be fully justified in putting it down: he was entirely convinced that the Gauls' animosity toward Rome was endemic in Lugdunum Convenarum. It was an ulcer that needed to be drained.

"Your daughter isn't here, Hadrianus. Is she not feeling well?"

"No, Rufus. She didn't want to witness the execution. She stayed home."

Valerius, sitting next to him on his left, didn't budge but Hadrianus felt his accusing eyes upon him.

"Could it be that she, too, harbors some feelings for the Gauls?"

Hadrianus made no reply: the inference was clear. For Rufus his friendship with Gedemo was a form of guilt. Still he tried once again to salvage what he could of the alliance between the Romans and the Gauls.

"Isn't this a little hasty?"

"Hasty, what do you mean, hasty?" Rufus retorted with fake naiveté.

"Why rush into these executions: Shouldn't we take some time?"

"So that the Gauls don't have time to start thinking that Rome is weak and that its justice can be scorned."

"But why put them to death here? Executions usually take place in the nearest amphitheater. You could have sent them to Tolosa or to Narbo so that they would die as patricians must die, killed by the lions or the gladiators."

"It's to prevent you from trying to appeal to the Proconsul or the Consul in Rome to save them."

As he said this, he turned to him with a smile:

"Don't worry, I am doing what you should have done from the beginning, right after Cracius was killed: I am going to show the Gauls what happens when they harm Romans and I'm going to show the Romans that a Convene can never be trusted. That's why they will hang here, in Lugdunum Convenarum, for all, Romans and Convenes, to see."

A decurion had placed each prisoner on a three foot high block, facing the crowd, and strung the rope around their necks. The ropes were hanging from a horizontal beam supported by two enormous tripods, roughly hewn from large tree trunks. The scaffold looked oddly rustic against the fine stone background of the thermal baths.

Gedemo, naked to the waist, his majestic face lifted to the sun, seemed invincible. His sons, like his nephews and even Dorix were of a heavier build but it was he who radiated the greatest strength.

None of the Convenes showed any fear but they offered no resistance, not out of a sense of resignation but as a last challenge to Rufus' authority: they wanted to show the Romans who the real barbarians were.

The crowd swayed and pushed against the row of legionaries holding back the Convenes whose anger was growing. Romans and Gauls had spontaneously chosen to stand at opposite ends of the scaffold and the platform: they looked like two walls about to fall against each other. The people of Lugdunum Convenarum all realized that from this day on, things could never be the same between the two peoples.

Rufus was oblivious to this but Valerius was alarmed. He looked at Marcus Satigenus who was walking through the ranks of his men, giving orders to his decurions. The legionaries were nervous. The city's garrison had stayed back, standing behind the rostrum, ready to move in whenever Valerius signaled. As for the Propraetor's personal guard, it deserved its name as never before: it was literally glued to him, since danger could come from all sides.

The decurions signaled that the six Convenes were ready. Marcus walked back from the gallows to the podium; he climbed the few steps and took his seat next to Valerius.

Suddenly, there was complete silence. The time had come. Everyone held their breath. No one believed that Gedemo was guilty, not the people, not the nobles, not even the soldiers; still, nothing could reverse Rufus' decision. Valerius was surprised by the sudden hush. Would the Convenes react at the last minute to try and save their leader, or avenge his death, or would they let him be sacrificed so that peace could return and they could be rid of Rufus Riego? He couldn't make out their intentions. They probably didn't know themselves what they should do. Was the honor of their people worth more than its future as part of the Roman empire? Rufus Riego stood up and read out the sentence. The moment seemed unreal: Gedemo and Rufus, alone, facing each other.

Valerius Musa didn't listen; he caught a few words that echoed across the forum; Gedemo was probably also not listening. The words made no sense: "Balbius... murder... Rome... magistrate... guilty...death..."

The words that echoed in Valerius' mind were altogether different: "The long-haired ones... love... betrayal... revenge... innocent... Staia...Staia Trevia." In his mind, he tried to get away from the sorry scene unfolding in the forum and the throng of spectators. He thought of the peak, high up in the hills, where everything started, where Staia had probably lain in wait for Cracius and caught him when he paused under the oak, after his night with Epotsorovida. It was easy for her to hide in the little grove half way up the peak. Did she try to talk to him, did she ask him to explain? Maybe she cried, maybe not.

Again, he tried to picture the scene, but, suddenly, something stopped him: something had stirred in the crowd, on the Roman side, and the spectators parted and let through a small, frail figure.

Rufus had seen it too. He had finished reading the sentence and was about to give the decurion the order to kick out the block under Gedemo's feet, when an astonishingly strong voice came from the little figure: there was so much authority in that voice that Rufus' hand was stilled.

"Stop!"

A whisper ran through the crowd, like a wave of palpable sound: it began with that woman's determined command and was borne along like ripples spreading around a stone cast in a pool of water.

"Gedemo is innocent. I'm the one who killed them!"

There was more murmuring in the crowd. Some people couldn't make out what she was saying. What was this about?

Hadrianus was standing on tiptoes to see better: he had not recognized his daughter at first. Horrified, he whispered:

"Staia. Staia, don't!" As if she were still a child.

Rufus was crimson with rage.

"Your daughter? This is your daughter! I'm warning you, Hadrianus, if this is one of your tricks to create confusion and save Gedemo, you will pay."

The Propraetor had been savoring in advance the effect the execution was certain to have on the people. They were to witness Roman justice in action. It would be a moment of glory for him. Now, just as the drama he had staged was reaching its climax, everything was ruined. He shouted to one of the decurions standing at the foot of the platform near Staia:

"Decurion, arrest this madwoman, take her away! And you, proceed with the execution, what are you waiting for!"

"But, I…"

The decurion was confused and pointed to Staia; Rufus' anger grew.

"I'm in charge here. Proceed with the execution!"

"No! Wait."

The decurion froze again. This time, Valerius Musa had spoken. He had come down from the podium and was walking toward the soldier with his palm outstretched, ordering him not to kick out the block. Rufus couldn't believe the centurion would dare interfere.

"You dare to oppose me?" he said slowly. The threat in his voice was so palpable that everyone on the podium froze.

"Let us at least wait until we hear her out. You must listen to her, Rufus."

The legionaries were holding Staia but she continued to struggle and screamed:

"I'm guilty. Throw me in prison, hang me…I don't care; just set these men free. They are innocent."

Her voice failed her; she struggled with all her might against the legionaries who restrained her like a little wild animal. In the crowd, the whispering had turned loud. People were asking their neighbors what Staia had said and were repeating her words. Infuriated, the Propraetor screamed his orders to the decurion over Valerius' head but the soldier, seeing the Convenes stirring, hesitated.

"Hang him. Its' an order, or else you'll be the one to hang."

But Rufus couldn't finish his sentence: Valerius had seized him by the collar of his toga and held his sword to his neck. There was a cry of fear: at the sight of the weapon everyone on the podium stepped back.

"Can't you see what's happening? You made a mistake, Rufus. You are going to listen to what she has to say, whether you want to or not."

Everyone in the crowd was watching the scene but it wasn't possible to understand what was really going on: Hadrianus' daughter interrupting the execution, screaming and struggling against the soldiers dragging her away, Valerius Musa threatening the Propraetor… They didn't know what to think, what to do.

Only Marcus Satigenus knew exactly what he should do: without a moment's hesitation, he drew his sword and plunged it into Valerius' side, piercing the lungs and driving straight to the heart.

It was so fast that Caius Retus had no time to warn Valerius. All he had time to see was, first, Marcus drawing his sword, then pulling it out of Valerius' side, and then blood gushing out and splattering his caligae and the edge of his tunic. What took place in between went by in a flash: he had no image of it.

Valerius, startled, stood for a few seconds, wondering why they were all looking at him, Rufus, Hadrianus, Marcus…

What was it that made him let go of Rufus? The answer was in their eyes.

His face twisted, his sword fell from his hand. He heard it slam on the wooden floorboards and rebound on the pavement below. He fell on his knees, first, and then backward. He heard the dull sound of his body hitting the floor, but he felt no pain; only inside, deep inside his chest, did it hurt. The blood ran. As life ebbed out of him he could still hear Staia scream her hatred of men and her pain:

"I have the lock of Epostorovida's hair; I took it from Cracius' body when I killed that dog; I killed him and I killed all the others. May their souls wander forever and never reach the gods' resting place."

She managed to free an arm from the legionaries and seized the lock of hair she wore in a satchel tied around her neck and threw it over their heads. It flew up in the air and fell right inside the empty space between the gallows and the podium.

Staia broke into a mad laugh that made the crowd stand back.

"I would kill you all if I could. May Pluto take your eyes away."

She was seized with convulsions; her head jerked back; it looked as if she might escape the soldiers' hold. People standing close were frightened and began walking away. The legionaries finally carried her off but her frenzied laughter still echoed in the forum.

Everyone on the podium was standing now, dumbstruck. Claudia fell into her husband's arms and was beating his chest:

"Do something! You are the First Magistrate. Say something! This isn't true, it's a plot, they've drugged her."

The Vespasiani, the Iassi, the Melalae, the Bassei and the Senicae now surrounded them and their eyes were full of hatred. The lock of hair from the long-haired girl was irrefutable proof: it had never been found, only the murderer could have taken it. Dignified mourning had given way to the long suppressed venom of pain. The murderer was among them, Hadrianus and Claudia had raised the girl who killed their sons! Apronia Vespasiana burst into tears; Eumachia Melala shouted her hatred at Hadrianus. Meanwhile, he went on calling softly to his daughter as she was being carried away. His sons, Julius and Lucius clung to him and cried out as they saw their sister being dragged out of the forum like a madwoman. They could not understand what was going on but they knew something terrible was happening, something that threatened Staia, their father and their entire family.

"You raised a venomous snake. Now your daughter will suffer and die in shame; now you'll know what it's like to lose your own child!"

Claudia turned to Eumachia, her friend just a few minutes ago and shouted at her:

"You are talking to Hadrianus Trevius, a senator, of senatorial rank, the First Magistrate of Lugdunum Convenarum, don't you forget that!"

"I am talking to the parents of a murderess, a coward who killed our children. You are nothing anymore, Claudia, your family is nothing!"

Struck by the terrible words, Claudia grabbed her husband's arm, willing him to fight, to respond to the insult. But Hadrianus had given up; his daughter was lost, he had lost, he knew it. Eumachia was right.

All of a sudden, Claudia realized the truth: her husband had always parried an attack with a more powerful one but this time, there was nothing left to fight for. The prospect of dishonor struck her then in full force: she dropped down to her seat as if felled by a blow. An abyss had just opened under her feet. Just a few hours ago, she had been sitting languidly under the tingling sensual touch of the ornatrix doing her hair, as she heard the voices of the children playing in the peristyle. She was feeling sorry for Gedemo, she could not believe that he was guilty of the terrible murders and thought of the poor young men she had known so well and loved so much. Nothing could compare with the agony she was suffering now. What were they going to do to Staia, her little girl, her love? They would probably lock her up in the Mamertima prison in Rome. What would become of her family?

Meanwhile, the Convenes were demanding that their leader and the five young Gauls be freed: they were still standing on the blocks, the ropes fastened around their necks. Arms were raised, no show of weapons yet, but open threats: they were ready for battle, some calling for justice, others for revenge. Arms were raised against the sky, facing the podium and the Roman nobility.

The legionaries of Marcus Satigenus who were on the front lines closed their ranks but the crowd pushed back against them. Marcus tried to order the city's two centuries, who stood in back of the tribune, to move into position, but he had just killed their leader and it was clear to them that he had been wrong: revolt was brewing in their ranks too.

Rufus was speechless; he stared with an open mouth at the body of the man who had proved him wrong, who had made him fail. He was paralyzed. He couldn't feel any satisfaction that the truth had been revealed and that he now had the means to destroy Hadrianus through his daughter and rid Augustus of an old enemy. There was no triumph. What he saw in the dying man's eyes was his own downfall. Valerius' last words echoed in his mind: "You made a mistake, Rufus." The centurion was dying at his feet but he had won, the last word belonged to him.

Lorus Divolus saw the crowd pushing forward and the soldiers unable to hold it back. He knew what would happen if no one made a quick decision. He called out, several times, to the Propraetor, asking him what he wished to do now; shouldn't the prisoners be freed? There was no answer. He realized that no one, not Caius Retus nor any of the Roman nobles standing on the tribune was prepared to take action, so he decided to risk everything. He walked to the edge of the platform, took a deep breath and, he who had never been trained in public speaking, tried to make his voice sound assured and loud:

"Convenes, I am speaking to you in the name of Propraetor Rufus Riego. Listen to me."

He had to repeat the two sentences three times before the anger in the crowd subsided and they could hear him. He shouted, once more:

"Convenes! I am speaking to you in the name of Propraetor Rufus."

The Propraetor didn't react, so he went on:

"He asks your leader, Gedemo, Dorix and Brennos, and his three sons, Bellovese, Lutarios and Vallorix, to forgive him for the terrible ordeal he has put them through."

Rufus emerged from his contemplation when he heard the word "forgive" and he was going to silence Lorus but the manager stopped him with his hand. The Convenes had stopped pressing forward. They were listening; he couldn't understand why but it was a fact: his plan seemed to be working. Rufus decided to let the manager continue.

"We needed to do this in order to unmask Staia Trevia. The Propraetor knew she was guilty and that she would come forward and confess if she saw that innocent lives were at stake. So Rufus Riego set up this trap and she was caught. Staia will be punished, she will be sent to Rome and the Emperor himself will decide her fate. But the real culprit here is Hadrianus: he knew all along but hid the truth and let the Convenes be accused."

At first, Hadrianus couldn't believe his ears. Lorus Divolus, that lousy backstabbing traitor. For years he had endured the man's unbearable presence, his slimy obsequiousness, he had trusted him entirely. But all that time, this worm had been waiting for the moment when he could strike him in the back.

"You vermin; go back to the dunghill where you belong. You miserable swine."

All of a sudden, he spat in Lorus' face. The manager wiped off the spittle and said:

"That's all you have ever given me, but it's the last time I am wiping your slime off my face."

"You should thank me, you bastard, you son of a bitch. If it wasn't for me, you would still be a slave. I freed you and this is what I get. You should be grateful."

"Grateful? Really? You're the one who should thank me. I served you faithfully, day and night, for years. I did my work and I did yours too, I took care of the city business and of your own business: I helped you rebuild your fortune. But what did I get for my efforts? Not a single bonus, never a regular salary. Only thanks to foraging and gifts was I able to feed my family. To you, I'm still a slave, I manage the city but I'm just a freed slave who never gets invited to banquets because I don't have noble blood."

"So that's it! You would like to become an honestior, but that's not something you can buy. I will be remembered as the father of a murderess, but you, you will be remembered as a traitor and branded by infamy."

Lorus smiled; Hadrianus' insults were a balm to his wounded ego. He was so happy to be a witness to his master's fall; it was almost happening too fast to be properly enjoyed.

Claudia was destroyed. An immense feeling of sadness was added to the humiliation and the horror of what had happened. She was already resigned and together with Lucius and Julius, she cried.

The Convenes were in turmoil. Rufus sensed it. Lorus' words had put an end to the hostility but had sown confusion; he had had time to recover completely. His fighting spirit was back: he had to seize the opportunity, while the Convenes were hesitating, and take control. He walked to the edge of the platform and gave the long awaited order:

"Free them!"

Immediately the prisoners were untied. The crowd stepped back as they were freed and drew away from the legionaries. The soldiers dropped their spears slightly and rested their arms that were sore from holding them out straight against the crowd for so long. Rufus was distinctly aware of both camps heaving a great sigh of relief. Gedemo, Bellovese, Lutarios, Valorix, Dorix and Brennos, still disbelieving, walked over to their families and embraced them.

Canius and Flaccus, Valerius' decurions, did not take part. They left their ranks, walked over to their friend's body and lifted his head. He was still breathing but his eyes looked beyond the world of mortals. The legionaries of Valerius' two maniples came closer: they too wanted to see, and pay homage to their slain leader, but they were too many and Canius asked them to stand back. He stood up and looked at Marcus Satigenus, with his uniform stained bright red from Valerius' blood. Marcus stood firm, he had no regrets: Valerius Musa was a man who had lost the ability to not think that had made the Roman legion the best army in the world. People like him were a danger to the empire. It made no difference that he had been right in the matter of Gedemo and Staia; he had to be prevented from endangering the morale of the troops, now rather than later.

Valerius' legionaries stood there staring at him; two hundred pairs of eyes looked at him. Marcus spread his legs a bit more and with his fists on his haunches, stood ready to take on any of them.

For a very short moment, everything on the forum stopped, everything but Valerius' blood which continued to run over the city's heart, at the people's feet, on the pavement where he had so often walked. All those lies, all that ambition: what did it all matter now? He was leaving Rufus to his ghosts, Marcus to his certainties, Hadrianus and Staia to their fate.

He was leaving this world.

A mild wind was rising, the wind that blows in from the sea, all the way from the Latium maybe. Perhaps it carried a last farewell kiss from Serenia.

Valerius was smiling when his eyes froze.

The End